For my kids and grands—I wanted to
give you bits and pieces of your heritage.
Within these pages are glimpses of a
simpler way of life that I'm
profoundly sorry you will never know.
May there always be
hermit thrushes to sing for you.

For Ruth's family,
and all who loved her.
You know the truths;
please allow me the fictions.

Copyright © 2022 Margaret DiBenedetto
All rights reserved.
Published by Full Court Press,
Fleischmanns, New York

ISBN: 978-0-9905932-3-2
Library of Congress Control Number: 2022915488

No part of this publication may be reproduced, stored in a retrieval system, or transmitted in any form by any means, electronic, mechanical, photocopying, recording, or otherwise, without the written permission of the publisher.

For information regarding permission please visit:
thewildlifestories.com

Author: Margaret DiBenedetto
Editor: Laurie Lieb
Front Cover Illustration and Design: Fabia Wargin
Back Cover & Book Layout: Erin Papa

Printed in the USA

Silver Dollar Girls

A NOVEL BY
MARGARET DIBENEDETTO

Cokie,
It's a little book...
I hope you like it!
love,
Peggy

Her name was Teresa de Francisci. Her husband was a New York City sculptor who had emigrated from Italy. He'd been commissioned by the United States Mint to design the newest coin—the 1922 Peace Dollar—to commemorate the end of World War I. The engraving had to convey strength, yet still suggest the mercy and compassion of his adopted, beloved country. The young artist deliberated for weeks over the appropriate image. How could he best portray tough determination and, at the same time, grace and elegance?

CHAPTER ONE

Mae, March 2020

"Sit down," Max said to Mae after the last customer had left the East Village bar in lower Manhattan. "I need to tell you something."

He flipped the sign in the window and grabbed a couple of beers from the cooler. They sat at the bar.

"We're closing on Monday."

Mae couldn't believe it. "The day before St. Patrick's Day? That's crazy! It's our busiest day!"

"It's not up to us, Mae. It's COVID. The Health Department says bars and restaurants can only do takeouts, and Jerry decided not to stay open. He can't afford the extra expense, so he's shutting down till this blows over. He told me to pay you on Monday night. And he needs an address where he can send your tax stuff."

"Well, crap," said Mae. "What are we s'posed to do now?"

"I'm heading to Florida. If it's going to be shitty, I want to be where it's warm and shitty."

"Well, I'm not going to Florida," said Mae. "My parents are there. Damn. I've got to figure something out."

"What's up with your folks?"

"It's a long story," said Mae. "You don't want to hear it."

"Sure I do." He settled in with his bottle and Mae took a deep breath.

"I grew up in the Catskills, mostly with my grandparents, Oma and Buddy. Weekends we'd drive out to the farm where Oma grew up. Her parents, Gram and Gramps, still lived there. They had some cows and chickens, and I spent hours just roaming through the fields and wading in the stream. It was such a relief to be away from my folks. They argued all the time."

She quieted at the thought of Maggie and Cyrus. They must have thought kids were a real pain in the ass, because Mae never had siblings. But maybe it wasn't kids in general; maybe *she* was the pain in the ass. Maybe she was the reason Maggie drank so much.

"On the farm, I felt normal. I was happy. I played outside all day. I had chores. I learned how to drive the tractor. School was a big escape, too; I loved my teachers, and my grades were good. But then Maggie started drinking heavier, and Cyrus was high a lot, and they fought more, too. They never got physical or aimed it at me, but they were nasty to each other. It was loud. So I started staying at my friend Jenny's house on school nights. But one thing my dad did for me was that he drove me to Oma's every Friday and picked me up every Sunday. He even apologized to me once."

Mae took a long swig of beer. Tears came to her eyes and her voice choked up.

"He told me he was sorry he wasn't a better dad. He said deep down Maggie really did love me, she was just piss poor at showing it, and he wished it could have been different for all of us." She swallowed back the tremor in her voice.

"When I left for college, they moved to Florida so they wouldn't have to deal with the snow and cold and ice. In Florida they could snipe at each other in deck chairs year round on the back porch. I went to visit them a couple of times, but Maggie was always drunk. It was horrible."

"Jesus, Mae," said Max. "But you grew up okay, right? You're lucky it didn't really screw you up."

"I don't know if I'm screwed up or not, but I guess I survived," said Mae.

"So, if you're not going to Florida," asked Max, "where will you go? Can you stay with your grandparents?"

"Nope. Oma and Buddy are down there now, too. After Gramps died, Maggie hit bottom and Oma flew down to help. Then she decided to stay longer to try to get Maggie straightened out. And then Gram got sick. Buddy had stayed behind to take care of Gram, and then she passed away. Remember a few weeks ago I took some time off? We were so close. She made me feel loved, and safe. But she *was* 105. I miss her so much; it's strange that she and Gramps are gone . . .

"Anyway, it didn't make sense for Oma to fly back, and they decided not to have the funeral right then. I guess they'll have a memorial service after things settle down with Maggie. So two weeks ago Buddy drove to Florida. Gram was in the backseat in a 'simple, yet tasteful urn' from the funeral parlor."

"Jesus," said Max, as he shook his head.

"Yeah, Jesus," said Mae.

She walked back to the apartment in a fog. Her cousin, Gary, had let her stay there while he was in Europe. She'd only had to pay for the utilities, and she was grateful for the chance to live in the city. Damn. Without a job, she couldn't afford to stay in the city. And with everyone getting sick from this new virus, she *shouldn't*.

"Damn, Mae, options," she said out loud. "What are my options?"

She felt slightly surprised that she really didn't mind saying goodbye to Max. He was nice and he was a friend, but even though the sex was fun, they weren't very close.
So where could she go? As she'd told Max, not Florida. No way was she voluntarily jumping back into that mess. But where could she go?

Cold pizza again. She turned on the Channel 4 news. COVID appeared to be airborne and was spreading fast, but the scientists were telling people not to wear masks.

Are you kidding me? she thought. Even in basic microbiology we learned about facial barriers. Without them, nurses and doctors would drop like flies. Oh, right. If everyone panics and buys up all the masks, there won't be any left for hospital workers.

Mae cut up some T-shirts. As she started sewing, she thought about where she could go. By the time she'd finished the last mask, she had an idea. It might not be optimal, but it might be possible, at least for a while. She couldn't afford to rent a place, and she wanted to be as isolated from the new disease as possible. She called Oma's number in Florida.

"Hi, Oma!" she bubbled into the phone. "How are you? I miss you! I'm sorry I haven't called as often as I should."

After catching up, Mae told Oma her idea.

"Well," said Oma, "the house is in pretty rough shape, and it's been empty since Gramps died, but if you think you can handle it, of course you can stay there."

"Oh, great! Thanks, Oma! And is there any way you can get Jenny Grant's phone number and text it to me?"

"I'll call her grandmother when we hang up. And tomorrow I'll have the electric turned back on."

"Oh, Oma! Thank you so much! I didn't even think of that," said Mae. Then more quietly, "How're things down there? How's my dad?" She purposely never mentioned her mother. Ever.

"Cy's doing fine, Mae. He still has his job at the fertilizer plant, and he's trying so hard with your mom. He's a good guy, Mae."

"I know he is, Oma. Will you please tell him I say hi? And give Buddy my love? I'll call you after I get settled. And Oma, you have to be careful. Make sure you all wear face masks, and stay away from people, and don't go into stores. Order your groceries in, okay?"

The atmosphere at the bar was somber on Monday night. At closing time, the regulars said goodbye to Max and Mae; some gave Mae extra tips as they filed out. Max turned the sign in the window, then handed Mae a wad of cash.

"I thought this would be easier for you than a check, since you're heading out tomorrow," he said.

"Thanks for thinking of that, Max," Mae said as she hugged him for what she figured would be the last time.

"Take care of yourself, Mae. It was fun."

"Yeah, it was," she said. "You take care, too."

On Tuesday afternoon Mae packed her sneakers, jeans, and sweatshirts for the farm into her duffle bag. Nothing business or dressy. No heels, no fancy scarves. She folded her nice clothes into a carton and called Kim, the other waitress, who was about the same size.

Then Mae crammed everything from the bathroom cabinet into the top of her backpack and gave the little apartment a last going-over. She laced up her hiking boots. She slung her backpack over her shoulder, dragged her duffle bag and the carton of clothes into the hallway, and locked the door. She thought for a moment, bent down, tore open the box, and rummaged around. She found the cashmere scarf Oma had given to her and jammed it into her bag.

"Mrs. Santiago!" yelled Mae, as she knocked at the apartment next door.

The door opened a crack. It took Mrs. Santiago a moment to recognize Mae under the face mask.

"I'm going back to the Catskills," said Mae. "Can I leave Gary's key with you? And will you please give this box to my friend Kim? I told her she could pick it up tomorrow."

"Oh, sure, dear. I'm sorry you're leaving, you're such a nice girl. Good luck. Maybe you'll come back sometime?"

"Maybe someday," said Mae, "but please take care of yourself. Be careful, okay? Here's a mask. Make sure you always wear it in public, okay? Put it on even when your son comes to visit. And take care, Mrs. Santiago! Thank you!"

Mae headed for the train.

CHAPTER TWO
Ruth, March 1940

The belt of the 1938 Cub Trainer was tight across Ruth's slim frame. In front of her was the instructor's back. The low hangar buildings were lined at attention to her right and the spacious airfield was on the left. The instructor revved the engine and taxied the small plane to the chipped stone airstrip. He turned right and revved the engine louder, then started down the runway. Ruth's mouth was dry; she could barely breathe. Every nerve in her body tensed as the trainer picked up speed and hurtled toward the tree line at the end of the strip. At what seemed the last possible moment, the plane lifted into the air, cleared the trees, and climbed above the roads and buildings below.
Ruth had dreamed of this moment since she could remember; had tried to imagine what it would feel like. Now she knew: heaven. It felt like heaven.

When Ruth was six years old, a persistent buzzing sound lifted her eyes to the sky. She watched with wonder as a small plane passed not more than 200 feet over her head.

"I want to do that," she'd felt in her being, and she might have said: "I *need* to do that."

Through the years, that plane was vivid in her mind. She knew in her soul that she had to fly.

But how? Born the last in a string of nine children, she

knew there was barely enough money to feed everyone, let alone splurge on something as expensive as flying lessons. At 16, Ruth graduated from high school and went to work. She was determined to save enough money to learn to fly.

Early each day, Ruth climbed into the dairy truck with her dad and helped him deliver milk, cream, and butter to the village of Woodstock. Opportunities for time alone with him were rare and wonderful, and Pop trusted her with adult responsibilities. She balanced the ledger book, loaded heavy cases of glass bottles, and backed the truck down their long driveway. She collected money from their customers, who often left notes with directions and requests—which days they wanted how many bottles of cream, why did you leave too much butter last time, and how come you didn't know we weren't home for two weeks? Some of the notes were completely illegible, and some were in creative verse. Others were drawn as cartoons, and some made no sense at all. Ruth kept the most remarkable ones in an old scrapbook.

Most afternoons, Ruth walked down the road to Deanie's, the best and busiest restaurant for miles around. As a waitress, she had to move fast and be diligent. She needed to joke with diners and make them happy. She learned to make split-second decisions and how to work under pressure. Her customers always tipped her well. But even with both jobs, Ruth knew there was no way she could earn enough for flying lessons on her own. She had to come up with another plan.

So Ruth did the only thing she could think of—she went to the owner of the local airfield and proposed a trade. Could she please, *please* work around the airport in exchange for lessons? Mr. Hasbrough thought for a moment as he considered this wisp of a girl with fierce determination in her eyes. Then he said sure, he'd give it a try.

That day had been the best one of Ruth's life, until now. Now she was actually up in the air, and all she'd had to do was to show up at dawn and help pull planes out of the hangars. In the afternoons she'd scrub them down and help push them back in. It wasn't easy, but she enjoyed hard work and was thrilled to be working with airplanes. Her dream was coming true. She was making it happen, all by her 17-year-old self.

The plane soared, gaining slow, circular altitude until it leveled off. The roads and buildings beneath were barely visible.

"Look up ahead," the pilot yelled to Ruth. "See those railroad tracks? If you ever get disoriented, follow rivers or railroad tracks to figure out where you are."

Ruth could see the long, straight rail line hugging the Hudson River and another that veered westward toward her home in the Catskills. She gasped as the plane suddenly banked and plunged 200 feet toward the ground. Then the pilot pulled up the nose and leveled off.

"What'd ya think of that?" he yelled to her, expecting she'd react like most first-timers, airsick and in shock. She surprised him.

"That was wonderful!" she yelled back. "Just wonderful! Can we do it again?"

CHAPTER THREE
Mae, March 2020

Mae stepped onto the train. She found an isolated seat and glowered other riders away. Some were masked, but most weren't, and she imagined COVID germs floating around the car. She was feeling paranoid and hoped that maybe the sight of her mask would keep people away. No one sat near her.

She'd hesitantly called Jenny the night before. Jenny, who'd been her best friend, though Mae hadn't seen or bothered to contact her in years. Jenny, who had two little ones to put to bed, who had to get up early in the morning to teach third grade. Sweet Jenny had said "Wait a minute" and asked her husband if he could take care of the kids. Yes, of course he would, and of course Jenny would be there at seven when the train pulled into the Rhinecliff station. Mae felt horrible for asking and was relieved at the answer. She had no one else to turn to.

Near Poughkeepsie she pulled out her phone and sent Gary a text: "I'm headed to the farm. Thanks for everything. Mrs. Santiago has your key. Stay safe."

The train picked up speed. Mae felt a moment of concern; she couldn't remember where she'd put the envelope of cash. She pawed through the pockets of her back-pack. There were too many compartments to keep track of. She had tossed things in without thinking. She remembered taking out twenties to pay for the train ticket, but what had she done with the envelope? Panic mounting, she unpacked almost everything into her lap before she found it.

Jesus, Mae, she thought to herself. Get a grip.

She tried to be more organized as she repacked.

As they pulled into Rhinecliff, Mae snugged up her mask, grabbed her backpack and duffle bag. She stepped off the train and started down the steps. She stood for a moment looking at the cars in the parking lot.

Tightening her hood against the light rain and chilly breeze, she had almost turned around to wait inside the station when a little green Honda pulled up. The trunk popped open and Jenny got out of the car with a big smile.

"Hey, it is so good to see you!" said Jenny as Mae dumped the duffle bag in and closed the trunk. Jenny moved toward her for a hug.

"Oh, sorry, wait," Mae said as she backed away. "Can you put this on?" She handed Jenny a face mask. "I made it for you. Sorry about not hugging. This COVID thing is just kind of freaking me out."

"Oh, yeah, no, I'm sorry," said Jenny. She put the mask on. "No, it's okay. Probably a really good idea. But it's just so good to see you—it's been a long time."

The two hopped into the car. They talked nonstop as they drove along the charming tree-lined main street of Rhinebeck and veered west to cross the bridge over the Hudson River. The school where Jenny taught would be closing at the end of the week; she'd have to teach her class online from home.

She didn't know how that would work out with her daughters needing her attention and naps, so she'd asked her mom to come stay and help out. They talked about how life was pretty much the same in tiny Welby, but that some things had changed farther down the road in the larger town of Fremont. More people had moved up from the city, and there was a new coffee shop and a bigger grocery store. But at the old corner bar, the same characters were sitting on the same bar stools. Every few years the old drinkers were replaced with new drinkers. Same guys, just 20 years younger.

"There's still not enough to do, is there?" asked Mae.

"Nope," said Jenny. "Nothing but bowling, and drinking, and now Oxycontin. It's scarier than it was when we were growing up, Mae. Makes me really worry about the girls."

"Oh, damn." Mae turned and looked at her friend. "I didn't even think about that. Damn." She looked out the window into the dark and thought about her mom. She hadn't thought about her for a while. Was Maggie using opioids? And what a huge burden Jenny must feel as a mom, trying to keep that crap away from her little girls. What a hard time to raise children. Even with whatever was coming with the COVID epidemic, at least Mae didn't have to worry about kids. Compared to Jenny, Mae had it easy.

As they approached Kingston, Jenny said, "Okay, groceries. Where to?"

"Whatever's quickest. I don't even know what's around."

"Hannaford and Pete's are the quickest. But Aldi's is the cheapest."

"Aldi's it is, then. I don't have a lot of cash."

"Aldi's, here we come," said Jenny, and took the exit.

An hour later, they were headed west again, toward Welby. The small state highway wound through the mountains and, occasionally, tiny villages. The road was dark but clear of snow and ice. Mae and Jenny both watched for deer that might cross in front of the car.

"Ben went over to the house this afternoon, Mae. He turned the water back on and checked the chimney and started the wood stove. But it might be out by the time we get there."

"Oh, right, I hadn't even thought about heat and water. That was so nice of him, Jenny. I don't know how to repay you guys for helping me."

"Nah, don't worry about it, Mae. Someday you can watch the girls."

Mae was grateful to her friends. She'd assumed she'd just walk in and the place would be the same warm place she remembered. Without Ben's forethought, she'd have been in trouble.

Mae was also grateful that Jenny hadn't held the long period of silence against her. Since high school, Mae hadn't called or even sent an email to Jenny. She'd pretty much ignored her.

"Um, Jen," she said, "I want to apologize for not being in touch with you for so long. I used to hang your Christmas cards on my refrigerator so I could see how big the girls were getting every year. I was always going to send you an email, but I never got around to it. I think I stopped being 'responsible' after high school. I was tired of having to be the grown-up in the room. I was tired of being in control of every decision that affected me. I guess when I got to college, it felt like I had a chance to behave like a kid before I became an adult. So I let a lot of things slide. But our friendship shouldn't have been one of them."

"Listen, Mae, it's not a thing. Really, it's not. We both went in different directions. It happens. Sometimes I'd see Oma in town, and she filled me in on what you were doing. I kinda thought you'd be back one day, and now you are, and I'm really glad."

Jenny turned the car down the long, familiar road that led to the old Griffin farm. Mae realized that in a few minutes Jenny would drive away, and she'd be on her own. Even in the city, in Gary's apartment, she'd felt protected. With a secure place to live, an adequate job, and a few friends, everything had been neatly laid out for her. Now, for the first time in her life, Mae would be on her own. All alone.

"It's colder than I thought it would be," said Mae. "And there's snow!" Even in mid-March an inch of snow covered the ground, and the headlights reflected patches of ice on the dirt road.

"It'll get colder than this," said Jenny. "Let me know if you need more winter clothes. Oh, I almost forgot. Ben said he put the key back on the hook under the eave where he found it."

"Isn't it funny, Jen?" asked Mae. "Any place else, everybody's worried about somebody breaking in and stealing their stuff. Here, everyone knows where the keys are. It feels good to be back."

She grabbed her bags and Jenny started to carry in the boxes of groceries. Mae's hand instinctively reached for the light switch on the kitchen wall. The bare bulb cast the room in cold light; shadows played at the edges of the table and chairs. The room was smaller than she remembered.

When Jenny drove away, Mae walked through the downstairs. The rooms felt so familiar, yet so different. Years of no life in a place changed it. The furniture and doors and stairs, even the dishes and books of a lived-in house had souls, somehow absorbed from their owners. But when they'd been alone for a while, they reverted back to objects. And Mae could feel it. Everything felt different from when Gram and Gramps had lived there.

Ben had left a few pieces of wood beside the stove.

Better add some more, she thought.

She opened the door and immediately smoke came pouring out. She slammed the door shut.

Oops. Forgot to open the flue.

Years ago, Gramps had shown her how to load up the stove and start a fire and keep it going, and now his words came back to her. She turned the lever to open the flue, then opened the door. Much better. A small log still burned among the ashes. She loaded the rest of the pieces in, closed the door, and waited a few minutes to make sure the fire caught before she turned the lever back.

Her stomach growled and Mae realized she was hungry. She plugged in the refrigerator, unpacked her groceries, then took some of her newly bought paper towels and wiped dust and mouse droppings from the counter. She took a plate from the cabinet and rinsed it off. She noticed that the little white eggcup was still on the shelf above the sink. It had been there since she could remember. For some reason, Mae's spirits lifted, knowing the cup was still there.

She ate her sandwich at the old table that had been in their family for generations. Mae remembered Gramps sitting there, so appreciative of Gram's good cooking. She and Gram had sat there, too, playing cards and talking. She looked out the window and realized how quiet and still and totally dark it was. The nearest neighbor was almost a half mile away; the only lights on her road spilled from the windows of the old farmhouse and thousands of stars in the sky.

Mae found sheets in the closet of the little bedroom next to the kitchen. They had been placed into a plastic bag with pillows and bath towels and tied tightly against the mice. She made up the bed and put the clothes from her duffle bag into the dresser drawers and plugged her phone charger into the outlet behind the bed.

She wiped out the medicine cabinet above the bathroom sink and put her makeup, toothbrush, and a box of tampons on the shelf, and thought, *I'll need them soon*.

The envelope of cash—all she owned in the world, all $325—was at the bottom of the backpack. She took it to the bedroom and tucked it into the top drawer under her socks.

Great hiding place, Mae. First place anyone would look, she thought.

Suddenly, she straightened. She grabbed her backpack and went through all the pockets. *Her phone!* Where the hell was her phone? She reached into every compartment, knowing it wasn't in any of them. Had she left it in her jacket? She ran to where it hung in the kitchen and felt the pockets. Empty.

Oh shit, she thought. *ShitshitSHIT!*

It must be in Jenny's car. It must have fallen out of her backpack. Well, there was nothing she could do about it now. In the morning she'd have to walk to . . . where? Someplace she could call from. The Allen farm was the next place over; she could walk there tomorrow and give Jenny a call.

"Aargh!" Mae groaned. She didn't know Jenny's number—it was in her phone. But somehow she'd get it.

"Don't worry, Fifi," she could hear Gram saying. "You'll figure it out."

Mae felt a little better remembering Gram's steady voice and the funny nickname Gram called her.

Still subdued and disappointed, Mae got ready for bed. She reached to turn out the light, hoping that any mice coming in from the cold would scurry quietly and not wake her up.

Her dream, that night, began in the little apartment she "rented" from her cousin. They were on the couch and he said she'd have to pay more than just the utility payment; he wanted $5,000 a month. "Okay, Gary, I'll get the money," she said, and then she was at the bar, telling Max she needed a raise so she could pay her rent. Max told her no, all the money was gone, so they lay down behind the bar and made love. "But I'm just your friend," she told him. "I don't want to marry you." She opened the door and walked into the stream at the farm and waded through a cool, still pool and reached under the large rocks. Her hands closed on a big, muscular trout but she was not quick enough and it wriggled away. Gram's old dog Blackie barked at her from the bank, and suddenly Mae was on the tractor, squeezed onto the seat next to Gramps. He sang old songs to her and the notes of the music encircled them like a halo. They sat at the kitchen table and Gram and Oma piled food on their plates: pickle sandwiches and mashed potatoes and a big roasted turkey, and pies stacked in a tower, so many kinds of pies that they couldn't see over them.

Then she was little, five or six, sitting on Gram's lap in the rocking chair. Mae was crying, but Gram wiped her face and kissed her head and said in a pink and yellow voice, "It's okay, Little Fifi. You'll be fine, my love. Someday, you'll find your wings and fly."

And then Mae was 11, playing in Gramps's car with Gary and her arm hit the shifter and the car started rolling backward and it went faster and faster backward down the hill and she and Gary looked at each other with wide eyes because they knew they were in big trouble, and the car stopped when it crashed into the barn. Gram was at the car window, mad and yelling "Damn it, Fifi, if you're going to crash the car, I'd better teach you how to drive!" and then she started laughing and they all laughed and she gave them chocolate chip cookies. Then Mae was at college and Gramps died and she was at his funeral and felt such profound grief that even in her sleep tears streamed down her face onto the pillow. She ran from the funeral to the farmhouse and watched Buddy pile Gram's things into a little boat, and then Gram got into the boat and floated away, and the farmhouse was empty and lonely and sad. Mae lifted her arms and they were wings and she soared into the sky, circling high over the fields and the forests, and then turned toward the Hudson River. Then back on the ground she boarded the train and called her roommate to say she was leaving college and would never be back.

Mae bolted upright in the dark. Within moments she relived all the emotions of the dream—the sex with Max, riding on the tractor with Gramps, Gram's warm kitchen, the fun of crashing the car, the sorrow of Gramps's death and Gram leaving the farm, the surprise of flying, and then finally the shock that had woken her. She'd left college, *left college*, to selfishly move to the city so she could have fun, when everyone at home was counting on her to make something of herself. To do something special. And she'd let them down— Oma and Buddy, Gram and Gramps, even Cyrus. She was the first one to make it to college, and after Maggie, *especially* after Maggie, they had counted on Mae to realize her potential, and now she knew that all she wanted was for them to be proud of her.

I could have done it, she thought, *I could have graduated from college, and I didn't. I'm 24 years old. What am I going to do with my life?*

She'd wasted the one big chance she had to do something. A feeling of shame kept her awake for hours, thinking and tossing and turning until exhaustion finally took over and her mind stilled and finally she slept.

Mornings in the city had jarred her awake with trucks and traffic and doors closing in the hallway. But here in the mountains, nature stretched and blinked, and bit by bit everything came gently to life.

In the gauzy time between hearing outdoor noises and thinking, Mae nestled deeper into the warm blankets and pillows that smelled of Gram and pie. Mae had forgotten the luxury of slow wakening. She barely heard the muted cooing of a dove in the distance. Then a crow landed in the tree outside her window and cawed, loudly and repeatedly.

First thing: put wood in the stove. Mae had spotted a small stack of firewood Ben had left along the side of the driveway. She pulled on her boots and jacket and went outside. The cold made her gasp, but the air was fresh and reminded her of her childhood. Ben had dug out the old wheelbarrow from the barn and left it by the pile of wood. She loaded it and wheeled it back to the house.

After she'd stoked up the fire, Mae was ready for a cup of tea. She found the old teakettle in the cupboard, filled it with water, and put it on a burner. She turned the knob. Nothing. The electric coil of the old stove didn't even get warm. The next burner didn't work either.

Third one's a charm, she hoped, and the next burner turned red. The last burner yielded nothing.

Oh, well, at least there's one. And the oven seems to work, but Gram used to say it was 50 degrees off. But too hot or too cold?

Mae's mood dropped as she remembered her phone. Maybe she should leave for the Allen farm to try to call Jenny. But without her phone, she didn't even know what time it was. She plugged in the old radio on the windowsill. A voice spilled out, announcing the eight o'clock news. She placed the batteries from her flashlight into the kitchen clock. It worked, and she rehung it on the wall. At least now she'd know what time it was. But it was too late to reach Jenny; she'd have already left for school. Mae would have to call her in the afternoon.

Might as well explore the house. She'd seen the downstairs last night. The small bedroom would be fine for her; the bed had turned out to be more comfortable than she'd remembered. The living room was the same as it had always been—the old worn couch was against the wall, Gramps's chair was by the window, and the little wood stove in the corner, just big enough to heat the downstairs. By the light of day, the room seemed less foreign to her—warmer, brighter.

Mae went up the stairway to the second floor. Gram's father, Mae's great-great-grandfather, had rebuilt the steps when Gramps and Gram moved in. His expertise was evident. The rich maple stairs were finely crafted, solid and simple.

Small bedrooms were at both ends of the short, wide hallway. The hallway had been Gram's sewing room. Many skirts and dresses, curtains, pillowcases, and even Oma's elegant wedding dress had come from the old sewing machine on the small table. Oma had also sat there, sewing school clothes for Maggie and baby sundresses for Mae. A lot of love had been stitched on that machine.

Mae felt heat rising upstairs from the wood stove, and she remembered what Gram used to do. In a cedar chest in one of the bedrooms, Mae found a green wool army blanket. She went downstairs and got a hammer and some nails from the tool shelf in the entryway that served as a mudroom. Oma's old barn coat was hanging by the shelf; it fit just fine.

Thank you, Oma, Mae thought. *I'll need this.* She slipped it back onto the hook.

Back at the landing, Mae awkwardly held the heavy blanket above her head and a nail in place with one hand, while hammering with the other hand. When it was finally nailed up, the blanket hung down and blocked the stairwell. The downstairs would stay much warmer, and Mae would burn a lot less wood. There was no telling how long into April or May the pile of wood would have to last. Springtime brought surprisingly warm days and then frigid nights, and she knew there was always a chance of snow.

Mae found Gram's cleaning supplies and started sweeping and scrubbing the kitchen. Apart from some mouse droppings, it wasn't as bad as she'd first thought. The bathroom was in good shape, too. Oma must have cleaned thoroughly before they'd closed up the house.

By afternoon, Mae was done with her housekeeping. She was hungry, and more than that, she needed to get outside.

There were pockets of deep snow on the shady spots of the lawn. Mae shivered as she sat at the picnic table. The air was chilly; even with Oma's jacket and a hat, she'd wrapped herself in one of Gram's old blankets to stay warm. But the angle of the sun was changing. Without a breeze, the sun was almost warm enough to encourage stirrings of crocus and daffodils, and a little hope in her soul. Red-winged blackbirds trilled in the swamp, and a few juncos and chickadees chirped and perched on nearby bushes. She ate a sandwich and drank some tea, then closed her eyes and relaxed. She'd missed sitting still with just the smells and sounds of the earth around her. Her thoughts slowed, her mind calmed, and she felt secure, or secure enough, for now.

Mae looked down at the crumbs on her plate. Food. She needed to sort out plans for her food. At the grocery store with Jenny, she'd bought five boxes of herbal tea bags, two dozen boxes of pasta, ten pounds each of flour and sugar, two hands of bananas, two dozen apples, two dozen eggs, two pounds of butter, two rolls of paper towels, the last six rolls of toilet paper on the shelf, four big jars of peanut butter, and three loaves of bread. Enough for a while, but sooner than she'd prefer, her supplies would run low. With no car to get to a store, only a limited amount of money to spend, and no desire to be out in public during the pandemic anyway, Mae would have to figure out how to make do or do without, just like Gram and Gramps's families had done during the Great Depression.

She should have bought more peanut butter. Mae could just about live on bread and peanut butter as long as she filled in with vegetables once in a while.

Bread. If she was going to have bread, she'd have to bake it.

Tea bags. Why hadn't she bought more tea bags? She'd have to ration them out. She could maybe get three cups of tea from each bag.

Rice. Why hadn't she bought some rice?

She could plant a vegetable garden, just like Gram used

to. It would be a couple of months before she could plant, and then several weeks before a few things would be ready to eat, but she could get by on dandelions and the other greens Gram had shown her, if she could remember what they were.

Maybe the Allen farm still sold eggs.

She thought maybe Gramps's old hunting gun might be upstairs, but would it still fire? And would she find ammunition for it? And would she even remember how to use it anymore? She'd been a good shot, but it was years since she and Gary used it to plink soda cans, and she wasn't sure what she would hunt for, this time of year. Was hunting season even open in March? *Probably not worth it,* she thought. *Too much trouble.*

At least there were lots of fish in the stream. She knew how to fish. If one of Buddy's rods was still around, she could dig worms and catch some trout. Fishing season started on April first. Two weeks away.

Mae realized she could get by. At least she'd try.

While Mae sat at the table thinking about food supplies, three miles up the main road Charlie Glantz hung up the phone. Charlie owned a water-bottling facility on the Allen farm property, where a very prolific spring produced a constant stream of sweet, fresh water. Although Charlie paid Casper Allen rent on the land, as well as a fair price for each gallon of water bottled, his biggest expense was the supply of half-liter plastic water bottles he had to keep on hand. As he contemplated the call he'd just received, Charlie broke into a smile. The Well-Drug Company Vice-President in Charge of Procurement had informed Charlie that he'd won the bid to supply 300 tri-state Well-Drug Pharmacy stores with bottled water. And Charlie had recently installed a $100,000 plastic-bottle-casting machine in anticipation of the contract. His relief at the awarded bid was substantial.

Charlie told his bottling manager, Juan Flores, to start making bottles. Juan was in charge of making the bottles and getting them filled. They'd need enough cases of water to load five semitrucks a week for the initial deliveries. Juan's team fired up the machine. The Welby valley, which had up to now only heard the sounds of birds singing, coyotes howling, dogs barking, and tractors farming the fields, would be subjected to the loud *thump thump thump* of the casting machine as it produced 250 plastic bottles every ten minutes.

What Charlie had not anticipated was that, due to the COVID hysteria, bottled water, along with toilet paper, would be flying off shelves and in short supply across the country. Juan would soon need round-the-clock teams to produce and fill water bottles for 15 shipments each week. Charlie's $100,000 investment was about to provide impressive returns.

Mae spent the afternoon outside. She found a shovel and a hoe and other old tools in the barn. She tried to turn over the dirt in Gram's old garden; the ground still held frost and was hard as a rock. It would be a couple of weeks, probably, before she could work the ground and get it ready for planting.

She wandered through the field down to the little stream and watched the clear, cold water churn and swirl between the rocks and under the patches of ice along the sides.

We called it a "crick." City kids would come up here and they called it a "creek", and we thought that was the funniest thing. Then I moved away and started saying "creek" myself. Now that I'm back, it's a crick again. Is one right, one wrong? Did they think I was stupid for saying "crick"? Did I ever, somehow, see myself as wrong, or inferior, for the way I talked or for having clothes that were a little ragged and worn? And did anyone ever guess what my home life was like?

As she walked back to the house, Mae thought about what kids accept without a blink, what they think is strange, and what makes them see differences as either bad or good. Did that have an influence on how she saw herself as she grew up?

Mae got back to the house and looked at the clock. By the time she walked to the Allen farm, Jenny should be home from school. Mae shoved some dollar bills into her pocket and headed down the driveway. The rusty old mailbox was still there, still proudly proclaiming GRIFFIN. Mae was surprised to find that the creaky little door still opened and closed, and remembered how big and proud and responsible she felt the summer she was six and given the chore of retrieving the mail. *Finally* tall enough to open the box and look inside, if she stood on her tip-toes.

"Hi, Mrs. Allen!" Mae called, as she saw a figure emerge from the door of the milk house. Patsy Allen was a round woman with a constant smile and a shock of white curls she tried to control in a bun on the top of her head. Casper was round, too, with a perpetual smile on *his* face. When standing side by side, they looked like a pair of garden gnomes.

Casper and Patsy had taken the farm over from Casper's dad 50 years earlier when they'd graduated from high school. Over the years they'd milked cows, sold beef cattle, and dabbled in meat goats. The hay not needed on their own farm was sold to other farms, and they had a little refrigerator in the milk house where folks could stop and buy eggs and milk. Four dollars a quart or a dozen; leave your money in the Tupperware.

"Well, Mae McCain!" said Patsy, when she finally recognized Mae under the face mask. "I haven't seen you in ages! What in the world are you doing here?"

"I'm moving into Gramps's and Gram's place. Here, I brought you this." Mae handed Mrs. Allen a mask. "I made a bunch of these, and it's really important that you wear one to keep from getting sick."

"Well, okay," said Patsy. "I'm not sure what's going on out there. But here, I'll put it on, just for you, honey. So what are you doing here, sweetie? I was real sorry when your Gramps and Gram passed away."

They talked as they walked up the driveway to the house. Mae explained about her job ending because of COVID and her decision to move back to the farm.

"But the reason I'm here right now is to ask if I can use your phone. Jenny Grant gave me a ride from the train last night to the house. But I can't find my phone—it must be in her car. I was wondering if I could give her a call? The only problem is that I don't have her cell number."

"Of course you can use the phone, Mae, but let's see. I'll call Jenny's mom right now and get the number for you. I saw Janice in the store just yesterday."

Eventually, Mae got through to Jenny. Yes, Jenny would look for the phone and drop it off tomorrow. And yes, she would pick up some yeast and ten pounds of rice on her way over.

Mae felt so much better when she hung up the phone. She wanted to call Oma, but didn't want to wear out her welcome with Mrs. Allen. She could call tomorrow after she got her phone charged up.

"Thank you so much, Mrs. Allen. I'm going to get some eggs from the milk house on my way out. And I almost forgot—does Lanore still deliver the mail? I need to leave her a note."

Mae headed back home with a dozen eggs and the assurance that yes, Lanore still handled everyone's mail with care and kindness, running packages up to the house if they were too big to fit in the box.

That night a cold front blew through, and the temperature dipped into the teens. Mae hadn't paid attention to the weather forecast on the radio and hadn't put an extra blanket on the bed. She woke before dawn. The fire had gone out and the house was cold. She crawled out of bed, pulled on one of Gram's old sweaters, wrapped the cashmere scarf around her neck, and went to the living room. There were still a few pieces of firewood in the woodbox next to the stove, but she knew they were too big. She shivered as she stepped into the mudroom. It was even colder than the rest of the house. She turned on the light and rummaged through the closet until she found the small hatchet she'd hoped would be there.

"Thank you, Gramps," she murmured out loud.

She hurried back to the woodbox, picked up a piece of wood, and sliced off several long strips of kindling. She opened the flue and placed some crumpled-up paper on the bottom, then ripped up a piece of cardboard she'd found in the kitchen. On top of the cardboard, she carefully crafted a little tepee of the kindling wood.

Matches.

Darn.

She hadn't even thought about matches. Ben had probably used a lighter when he started the stove, and of course would have taken it with him.

Oh, shit.

Well, she was awake now. She was grateful for the hot water coming out of the bathroom faucet when she washed her hands and face. She opened the medicine cabinet for her moisturizer and saw the box of tampons.

I'm going to need them soon, she thought.

There were probably enough for this month, but why hadn't she stocked up at the grocery store?

What am I going to do next month? I might have to do what women used to do—cut up old rags and then wash them out.

Mae got into her cold jeans and cold shirt and sweatshirt. She put on her socks and hiking boots and her jacket and hat. Then she made a cup of tea—cup number one from today's teabag. She sat at the table and watched the day begin. Along with a wind that had blown through the thin walls last night, the cold front had laid down a half inch of snow on the ground.

"Poor man's fertilizer," Gramps used to say.

Dejected. The first time at the farm. She hadn't felt this low even when she realized her phone was gone. Now she was cold, alone, and lonely—completely on her own. Having no matches made her realize that she had to provide everything for herself. And here in the country, that meant not just comfort, but survival.

As Mae finished her tea, she thought about the women who'd lived here before. Gram had certainly made do without any conveniences Mae was used to. And the woman who'd lived here before Gram, raising a family and farming with her husband, too—what was the name? Gram had mentioned them. Kopek? Kopettz? That woman didn't have indoor plumbing or electricity; she'd worked even harder than Gram.

"Well, Miss Fifi," she imagined Gram saying, "don't feel sorry for yourself. Think about what you're going to do, then get up and do it!"

Mae stood up, pulled on her gloves, and went for a walk. She wanted to explore the farm again anyway, and there was no reason to stay inside a cold house when she could keep herself warm by hiking outdoors.

The first place she went was down to the swamp. The red-winged blackbirds weren't singing as loudly today, she noticed. They sat on the branches of the pussy willows, feathers all puffed up, saving energy by staying still. Mae found the path that wound around the beaver pond. A thin layer of ice glazed the top of the water. The pond was full, the mud edges were thick, and a sizable beaver lodge stood at one end of the pond. Mae stopped and stared.

The beavers are still here! she thought. *I don't know why*

I'm surprised; of course they're still here. I assumed that everything had changed. Some things have, of course, but other things have just been going on the same for hundreds and thousands of years . . .

But still. Still, she was pleased to be surprised by the constancy of life here on the farm.

Mae hiked around the pond, across the fields, and up the pastures to the woods. The upper half of the farm was wooded. The lower portion consisted of level fields, good for hay and crops, with a clear, constant stream—the "crick"—running through the middle. The driveway, the swamp, and the beaver pond hugged one end of the fields near the farmhouse.

Farther up the mountainside behind the house were the old cow pastures. As Mae walked through the pastures, the smell and feel of the dust on the path came back to her. Back when the farm had cows, Mae's weekend job on summer mornings, and Gary's too, when he came over, was to move the cows from the barn after the morning milking up to the pastures, where they'd graze all day, and then herd them back to the barn again in the afternoons. It was easy work; the cows knew where they were going.

She remembered the time she and Gary left the gate open and the cows got into the corn field and trampled through half of it and chasing them back to the pasture trampled the other half. Gramps had been mad, but he never raised his voice.

He just shook his head and said what he said whenever something surprised or baffled him: "Well, I'll be go to hell."

Mae walked through the old orchard and remembered climbing the apple trees, because the sweetest, ripest apples were always at the top. She'd climb as high as she dared before the upper branches bent too much. One time Oma was under a tree, looking up at her, and Mae moved and the branch dipped, and an apple fell and smacked Oma right in the eye. But Oma didn't even cry out, though it must have hurt really bad. She had two days of headaches and a black eye for weeks.

Mae remembered the day Gary pulled big heavy rocks off the stone walls, trying to catch woodchucks with the old cow dog. Gramps was mad, and he made Gary put the walls back together. But he didn't yell; he just walked away, shaking his head and muttering, "Well, I'll be go to hell."

Beyond the pasture were the woods, which Mae loved the best. Where she found peace. As a girl, she'd take an apple and a sandwich and disappear for the day, hiking on old logging trails or bushwhacking through the undergrowth, somehow calmed by the trees. In the woods, she was small. She was not the center of attention, didn't have to answer to anyone, didn't have to hear anyone, didn't have to think or react or defend or pretend. In the woods she wasn't lonely, wasn't hurting; she wasn't Mae McCain from a screwed-up family.

In the woods, she felt like the tiniest part of her surroundings. The sounds of the birds and the wind, the smells of decomposing bark and moss and ferns: the ongoing growth and death of plant and animal life that make up a forest seeped into her soul. For as long as she could recall, Mae had disappeared into the woods feeling broken, then emerged content and complete and centered. She could not articulate what happened, or why, but she knew it was essential.

Now Mae hiked again up the old logging roads, overgrown with thorn bushes and beech saplings. The trek was more challenging than she remembered. At times the trail vanished altogether and she detoured around new underbrush. Mae instinctively wound her way through the trees, guided by the angle of the sun, the contours of the terrain.

She reached the rise of the mountain. Breathing hard, sweating, and getting a very good workout, she stopped and inhaled deeply, and again, as years ago, her brain shifted to a better place; her mind was still. Her breathing slowed. She relaxed.

When her stomach rumbled, she turned and made her way back down the mountain.

The sun shining through the windows had warmed the house. Mae put the kettle on for a second cup of tea and made a peanut butter sandwich and remembered once asking Gram to add a piece of lettuce. For crunch. She wished she had lettuce.

The house and the farm no longer felt strange or lifeless. They felt once again as they had when Gram and Gramps lived there, as though they had accepted her return, welcomed her back. She began to feel . . . *comfortable*.

And she felt better, too, knowing Jenny would come by in a few hours with the phone and extra groceries, and Mae could get a ride to the Allen farm for some matches or a lighter, and she would finally be able to start the wood stove.

At four o'clock, Jenny's car pulled up to the farmhouse. Mae came out of the barn, took off her work gloves, pulled a face mask from her pocket. From a distance they traded air hugs. Jenny grabbed a bag of groceries from the backseat and put it on the door step.

"Thank you so much, Jen! How much do I owe you?" asked Mae.

"Twenty'll do it. I got a few extras for you, too. But, Mae," she said, "your phone's not in my car. I've looked everyplace. I checked between the seats, in the trunk. It's not here."

"Oh, no!" Mae was stunned. Where the hell could it be?

"I'm sorry," said Jenny. "When was the last time you saw it? The last time you used it?"

"Okay, let me think. On the train. I called Gary—no, I sent him an email. Or did I send him a text? That was the last time I used it."

"Then what did you do with it? Put it in your jacket?"

"No . . . I would have put it back into my backpack. There's a special pocket for it. But it's not there. After you brought me here, I unpacked my duffle bag and my backpack, and it wasn't there."

"Oh, shit." They looked at each other, knowing Mae would probably never see her phone again.

"The train," said Mae. "It's on the train. I remember now that I couldn't think of where I'd put my cash, so I emptied the backpack on my lap and found the cash and then put everything back in. Oh, no, it must have fallen off the seat or something, and I didn't even think about it! Damn!"

Jenny promised to call Amtrak when she got home to report the missing phone.

"Um, you know, Mae," she said as she was leaving, "even if we find your phone, there's no cell service here."

"Of course not," said Mae. Her shoulders slumped.

Mae carried the groceries into the house, feeling more despondent than she had in weeks. She couldn't believe she'd done that. How stupid not to make sure she had her cell phone. *Shit. Just shit.*

The house was cold again. Clouds covered the sun and the wind had picked up. And she'd forgotten to ask Jenny for a ride to the Allen farm. Now she'd have to walk up there again to see if she could get some matches. *Shitshitshit.*

Mae started to unpack the groceries. At least now she had rice, and yeast.

Yay! I can bake bread!

Damn. She'd forgotten to pay Jenny. And now she had no phone, no heat, and life was shit. Goddamn it. Damn it to hell. And she thought of Gramps.

"Well, I'll be go to hell," she said out loud, and she felt a little better.

Mae looked in the bag. *Cookies! Yay!*

And olive oil, a small bottle of ketchup, and two more rolls of toilet paper. *Yay!*

And in the bottom of the bag was a small red and white box.

Containing 300 LiteEasy wooden matches.

CHAPTER FOUR

Ruth, April 1940

"Pop," said Ruth, as they hopped into the dairy truck. She hadn't planned to tell him. She thought she'd go to the airport like any other day, then tell them all when she got home. But she felt like she'd burst if she didn't tell him now.

"Pop," she repeated. "Guess what? Today's the day! Ray, my instructor, told me that I'm finally going to solo!"

Pop, ever thoughtful, turned and looked at his youngest daughter. A wide smile slowly spread across his handsome face.

"Well, son of a gun!" he said.

Throughout the morning he caught her grinning with anticipation, and she caught him gazing at her with pride. When their route was finished and they were walking to the house, he handed her a large silver coin.

"Put this is your pocket, honey. It's not for luck; you are the most careful and deliberate person I know. No, it's for courage. She's you, Ruthie. I look at her face and I see you."

Ruth took the coin and examined it. The girl on the front held her head high and gazed steadily at the horizon. Unruly tendrils of hair feathered around her face. She embodied calm, bold bravery.

"Pop! Oh, Pop," she said, and hugged her father tightly.

As she flew the route Ray had mapped out, everything

else fell away. The plane danced through the first low, wispy clouds, then angled higher toward a heavier layer. Ruth concentrated on the hum of the engine and the mild chop as the craft gently bumped up, then down, then up again. It pushed through the turbulence. To her, there was only the plane. The plane, and Ruth, who felt merely an afterthought, burst through the gray blanket into blinding sun. She turned the aircraft slightly until they—she and the plane—were no longer trapped by the brilliance, and her breath caught at the snowy cloudscape before her. Hills and tufts, flat-topped mesas and towering alps, whiter than white, confected from particles of dust surrounded by droplets of water. Ruth had not, until now, witnessed grandeur. She knew the word, but until now hadn't gotten its meaning. Now she understood that it stops your breath and nearly stops your heart, and she was conscious of nothing else. Her hand dropped to her pocket where she touched the rim of the coin. She traced the outline of the young woman's face and felt as though she and the girl on the dollar were sharing the spectacle together.

Ruth breathed deeply as if to inhale the moment, then dipped the plane beneath the cloud cover. Changing course, she headed northward along the Hudson River, then veered east toward the Berkshires, then southward again.

Eventually she circled back to the little airport. She searched the sky for oncoming aircraft and the ground for any that might be taking off. There were none, so she guided the plane into a shallow right turn, the "dogleg" that straightened her approach to the airport, and began her descent. The checklist ran through her mind: decrease throttle, stay firm on the brakes, keep the narrow wheel-base steady and tires on the ground as much as possible; remember that the Cub has a tendency to bounce.

Executing each step perfectly, Ruth taxied the plane down the airstrip to the front of the hangar.

As she walked toward the office, her head was still full of the wonder she'd experienced above the clouds.

It wasn't until her instructor exited the building and came toward her that she realized the other important part of the day.

"Great job, Ruthie!" exclaimed Ray, with a hug. "Congratulations! You're a pilot!"

CHAPTER FIVE

Wesley, March 2020

Wesley and Jack sat at the edge of the pond. The two looked into the water. The water was cold. Too cold to reach into for more than a few minutes, and Wesley didn't have his mittens.

"No salamanders today, Jack," said Wesley. "Maybe frogs?"

Wesley got up and tiptoed along the bank. Jack followed.

Wesley was six years old. He lived with his father in the house across the field. He couldn't remember his mother. He remembered something, though, a scent, or maybe a feeling.

Wesley stepped on a clump of grass that in the summer would have exploded with frogs leaping into the air and splashing into the water. Jack would have jumped in and tried to bite the little green bodies swimming away, doing his best to help Wesley. But today, before spring arrived, before the frogs even considered crawling out of the bottom muck, nothing stirred. Wesley was bored and kicked through the grass, hoping to prompt something out while Jack bobbled up and down beside him, focused and alert. Jack was Wesley's best friend, pretty much his only friend. Wesley's parents had gotten the black and white border collie when Wesley was born, and after Wesley's mom died, Jack did his best to fill the void he sensed within the little boy.

Wesley's dad, James, had great faith in the team of Wesley and Jack. Each day after breakfast, he sent them out to wander and play while he set up his sawmill to plane boards or sharpened his chainsaw to cut the immense piles of logs alongside his barn. He sold and delivered firewood, making just enough to thinly support the three of them. James knew that Wesley had sense, the pond wasn't deep, and the dog was faithful to the boy. He knew that when Wesley was hungry they'd show up again. James banked on the instincts of generations of kids who'd roamed and rambled and gotten back home alive. It was how he'd grown up; no reason his son couldn't do the same. As he worked, James kept an eye in the direction they'd gone, but he'd not yet had to go in search of them.

When he tired of looking for frogs, Wesley decided it was a good day for sticks. Not just any sticks; he needed them green and pliable and able to be stripped of their bark. Willows were too bendy, but young maple saplings stayed sturdy. Maple was hard to cut, though. He'd already worn down the sharp edge of the little penknife his dad had given him for Christmas. But Wesley knew that if he sawed long enough, he could get a sapling down. He cut four of them about a foot long; a good length, he thought, for effective swords. Then he stripped the bark with the dull blade and sharpened the ends the best he could. He had a pretty good supply so far, but it never hurt to have more. He kept some in his bedroom closet. Just in case.

If the knife slipped and cut him, Wesley had learned that if he sucked on the wound until it stopped bleeding and then stuck it in the mud, it would stop hurting and heal up pretty fast.

While Wesley added to his arsenal, Jack chased squirrels and snuffled through the underbrush for mice and moles.

As long as Jack was near, Wesley felt secure. He knew the dog would watch out for him. In addition to being brave, Wesley was smart; he knew he was just a kid.

CHAPTER SIX

Mae, April 2020

In the dream, Mae was in the barn and she was little again, maybe six or seven. Gramps was stripping out a cow's teat and the gray tabby sat in front of him. He aimed a stream of milk at it and the cat licked the warm white liquid from its chin and Gramps laughed when it opened its mouth for more. Then Mae was in front of the hay manger and the row of cows' heads stretched down the length of the barn. She rubbed the tufts of hair of the heads of the nicer ones and kept clear of the mean ones that tossed their horns. She slid the top from the barrel of molasses Gramps added to the cow feed and plunged her hand into the thick brown sweetness and licked the sticky syrup off, one finger at a time. Oma said she shouldn't do that—sometimes mice got in there and drowned—but she tried not to think about the mice and reached into the barrel again and put her hand into her mouth and sucked her hand clean, then pushed the top back on.

With the morning sun, the crow was constant and punctual and irritating. Mae didn't know why he was so faithful but he began Mae's days, and eventually she didn't mind getting up early. She liked a full day for chores and hiking around the farm. The fresh air, along with working in the vegetable garden and exploring the mountain, wore her out. She had begun to clean up the yard. Gram and Oma had been proud of the neat and orderly lawn and the tidy flower beds. Maybe Mae couldn't turn it into what it had been, but she could rake up the old leaves and remove the broken branches that were scattered around. At the end of the long days, she was in bed by nine, slept well, and woke feeling refreshed. She'd lost some weight, but her muscles were toned and she felt healthy. Except that lately her stomach was feeling queasy, and she'd given up breakfast.

Sitting at the table, Mae had a cup of tea; the first of her daily three. The news on the radio was about the press of COVID cases in the New York City hospitals. The governor mandated face masks in all public places and extended a stay-at-home order to the middle of May. Thank God, and Oma, that she'd had the farmhouse to come to. She loved it here, even if she was short on food and cash. Even if her new life was hard, and lonely. Every day Gram whispered to her, "You can do it, Fifi. Toughen up and do it."

Cup in the sink, floor swept, then out to the garden to dig up the patch of dirt that in a few weeks could be planted with seeds of arugula and kale, and what else?

I have to go into town and buy seeds.

But not now. She straightened her back and threw down the shovel. She headed to the forest.

Mae hiked up the rise and cut east across the mountain. She followed an old logging trail, more overgrown than the others, yet still clear enough to negotiate this early in the spring before the growth spurt propelled the berry bushes head high and brought up stinging nettles that launched painful attacks on thighs. Mae wound her way through the forest maze. She hadn't been on this part of the farm in a long time, but knew she'd cross two stone walls and then a third, which was the property line. From there, she could turn right and follow the wall to the top of the mountain, and then turning right again, she'd end up back behind the house. Gramps had told her she had extra magnets in her nose, because even when she was little, Mae was rarely disoriented and usually knew where she was. Even finding her way through the city hadn't confused her. One thing Mae never felt was lost.

She headed through a break in the first stone wall and stopped to take a long drink of water from the old deerskin bota bag she'd found in the closet. Slung over her shoulder, the bag was easier to carry than her metal water bottle, and by the time it was empty, it was weightless.

After the second wall, the trail wound past a pine grove that Gramps had planted when he and Gram bought the farm. She spied a patch of green leaves emerging from the ground.

"Leeks!" she cried out in delight.

Mae hadn't had leeks in a long time. Gramps and Buddy would take her up the mountain road in the old army jeep and they'd bring back buckets of them. Gram made gallons of potato leek soup and canned it for special occasions. And Gramps always saved some out for sandwiches. Nothing better than two pieces of bread smothered in butter and a few leeks in between.

Leeks, Mae thought, *the national symbol of Wales.*

She pulled a few of the fragrant, onion-y leaves from the

ground and jammed them into her pocket. Tomorrow she'd come back up to harvest more. The timing was perfect; her supply of vegetables was running low and the leeks would be growing for at least a month. Walking on, Mae thought it was strange that weekenders called them "ramps." She wondered if they thought it was strange that locals called them "leeks."

Up ahead, Mae spotted the third wall. As she got closer, she felt disoriented. There was bright sunlight where the forest should have been dark with trees.

"Oh, no!" she yelled and ran to the wall.

The trees that had stretched from Gramps's farm to the next farm, and then for miles down the valley, weren't there. Acres upon acres in front of her had been clear-cut and bulldozed. Spring rains had turned the exposed dirt into mud; the bare earth was zigzagged by deep, ugly, sludgy ruts. Mae was stunned. Why would the neighbor do that? Mae felt sad for the land; there was no dignity, no respect in what had been done. Tears came to her eyes, and she sank to her knees. She cried for the forest that had been sacrificed, the habitat that had been lost. Eventually, she knew, the land would recover and support life again. But re-creating the ecosystems would take years, even decades.

Mae rose to her feet. She turned and headed up the hill. She veered westward, out of sight of the desecration, then back toward the house.

Nothing went right that day. The shock and anger she'd felt at the sight of the clear-cutting blanketed her. Mae needed to work the blue feeling from her soul. She filled the old wheelbarrow with wood. It would be heavy; it was probably too full. She lifted the handles and finally got the wheelbarrow turned around, and started toward the house.

"Come on, Fifi, you can do it. Just get through this muddy spot and you're almost there," she muttered.

Mae struggled with the weight, then picked up momentum. And then the wheel hit a rock and jammed. The wheelbarrow stopped short, and Mae's feet went out from under her. On the way down her chin smacked the end of a piece of wood. *Wham!* The force of the impact spun the other end upward and the wood smashed into her nose.

Mae landed hard on the ground and lay still. She moaned and reached to touch her face. Her fingers were bloody. Blood poured from her nose. The skin on her face had been ripped and was bleeding too.

Damn. Her nose was probably broken.

Shit, she thought. *Shitshitshit!*

She willed the pain to go away. Then she knew it wouldn't. Tears streamed into her ears. She cried because of the pain and because she felt defeated. She felt sorry for herself. There was no one to care for her, no one to give her sympathy. She was alone, so she had to do it herself.

She finally roused up onto her elbows. Her face hurt, but at least she could move. She sat up, slowly got to her feet, and stumbled to the house.

Mae slept through the insistent call of the crow, but not through the noise of the phoebe who'd built a nest outside the window. The phoebe was a sweet little bird that was impossible to ignore. Its ridiculous *squeak-y, squeak-y* noise reminded Mae of a dog toy.

Mae realized that her nose hurt before she even opened her eyes. Then she felt the pain in her eye sockets and, finally, her head. She pulled herself out of bed and looked in the mirror.

Oh, shit, she thought. There was dried blood in her nostrils and a long, bloody scrape that started under her chin and went to the top of her nose. There was definitely a blue hue between her eyes.

Damn, I look like hell. But she knew she'd look worse in a few days when her eyes would be circled in black and blue and, later on, green. She put a tissue to her nose and started to blow, gasping at the pain. Dizzily, she made her way to the kitchen.

She sat at the table and had a cup of tea. First of three.

Jesus, she thought, looking out the window.

Is this really worth it? Worth it for me to be here?

She knew it was. She knew she couldn't have stayed in the city. Emergency rooms and hospitals were overrun with COVID patients. The city's streets were empty; no one ventured out. Mae couldn't imagine being cooped up in Gary's little apartment. And Florida would have been a disaster. No, the right place for her was here at the farm.

She heard Gram's voice in her head saying, "Just keep going, Fifi. You'll make it."

She thought about yesterday. As nasty as the fall with the wheelbarrow was, worse, much worse, was the discovery of the clear-cut. Mae feel even more deflated.

"Well, Fifi, what're you gonna do about it?" asked the voice in her head.

I don't know, Gram. Not yet. But I sure as hell can't sit here all day.

Moving hurt. Her body was achy, but Mae forced her arms into Oma's jacket and went outside. She'd skip the hike today, she thought, but she needed to move. She worked slowly and dug up a little more of the garden, thinking of the seeds she'd have to buy and the money they'd cost.

Then she eyed yesterday's carnage. Pieces of firewood were scattered near the overturned wheelbarrow. Mae picked up the wood and moved it into the house, a few pieces at a time, and then hauled the wheelbarrow back to the barn. She was disheartened and exhausted.

That's it, she thought. *I'm done.*

Walking back to the house, she absentmindedly reached into the jacket pocket and found the leeks she'd picked the day before. The pungent aroma made it through her battered nose and into her soul. Suddenly hungry, she went to the kitchen, spread two pieces of bread with precious butter, and placed the green leaves between them. She sat at the table and looked out the window. The sharp tang and sweetness blended together the hard and soft realities of life at the farm.

When Mae woke up the next morning, her body was stiff and sore. Her face looked decidedly worse, but her head ached less, and her spirits had improved. Yesterday's chilly wind had died and the sun was shining. Mae decided to walk to the Allen farm for some eggs. She'd begun to have an egg every morning with her first cup of tea. Soft-boiled, with a piece of bread, just the way Gram used to make. Gram would place the egg in the white ceramic eggcup, then slice off the top with a knife so Mae could spoon the warm, runny yolk from the shell.

People don't use eggcups these days, she thought. She smiled at how exotic the process had seemed.

Mae pulled a few dollars from her envelope and jotted a note to the mail lady. She grabbed a letter she'd written to Oma, picked up her backpack and her face mask, and walked to the mailbox. Gram had planted lilacs along both sides of the driveway, and over the years the bushes had grown to tower above the road. Their buds were just beginning to open, and in another month, their color and fragrance would be overwhelming.

Mae paused at the rusty mailbox to put the letter, some ones, and the note inside:

> Dear Lanore,
> Not sure if you remember me, but I am staying at my great-grandparents' farm for a while. In case I get mail I wanted to let you know that I am here. Can you please leave $3 worth of stamps?
> I hope you are well.
> Mae McCain

Mae turned up the road toward the Allens' farm. She heard a tractor in the distance—probably Casper plowing one of his fields. Just one car went past before she got to the farm. The sun was warm on her back, the stream next to the road was burbling, and the morning was peaceful. Mae began to feel happy.

Just before she got to the farm, a semitruck blew by her, barely slowing down. The wind whipped through her hair and dust from the road flew into her eyes. Oma had mentioned that the Allens had leased their spring out to a water company and that truck traffic along the quiet road was becoming a problem.

Damn, she thought. *Life's gotten too fast, even way out here.*

When she got to the farm, the barn was empty. So was the little refrigerator. Mae walked to the house, put on her mask, and knocked on the door.

"Hi, Mrs. Allen!" she said as the door opened. "I wanted some eggs, but there aren't any at the milk house. Do you have a couple dozen I could buy?"

"Oh, Mae, what happened to you?" Mae realized she'd forgotten about the black and blue circles around her eyes.

"I had a run-in with a wheelbarrow full of firewood," she said. "I think I look worse than I feel."

"Oh, honey," said Mrs. Allen, "do you need anything? Ice? Band-Aids? Aspirin?"

"No, thanks, just eggs if you have any. I ran out."

"Okay then. Yep, I was just taking some down to the barn. Let me get my mask. Here you go, two dozen."

Mae put the cartons in her backpack and handed Mrs. Allen eight dollars.

"Oh, I almost forgot," said Mrs. Allen. "Casper dug a bicycle out of the garage he thought you might want. It's old, but he says the brakes still work. He pumped up the tires and he thinks they're good. And here's my granddaughter's bike helmet—it's yours if it fits. Let's go see what you think of the bike."

They walked down to the barn and Mae tried it out.

"This is great!" said Mae. "Thank you so much. Please tell Mr. Allen I really appreciate it."

"You're welcome, Mae. And make sure you let me know if there's anything you need, okay? Be careful on the road—they drive those trucks way too fast."

Mae rode away. The brakes squeaked, but the bike worked. Mae started down the road, then looped around and back to the barn.

"Mrs. Allen, do you know if Mariella still makes tamales?"

"Yep, hon, I think she does."

"Great! Thank you!" Mae waved goodbye.

Having a bike changed everything. Now she could ride the six miles down the valley to the Kari-Out Gas and Convenience store when she needed something simple, like butter or matches. If she had enough energy, she could ride six more miles to the real grocery store in Fremont. Mae felt the wind on her face and remembered riding her bike on this road when she was a kid. She smiled all the way back to the farmhouse.

It was time to tackle bread. The store-bought loaves in her freezer would soon be gone and her meager supply of money meant that she'd have to become as self-sufficient as possible. One of Gram's old cookbooks had a basic bread recipe. The problem was that she'd watched Gram and Oma mix and knead and bake dozens of delicious loaves, but Mae hadn't paid attention to how they did it. Learning how to cook or bake or sew or knit wasn't nearly as much fun as playing in the crick or helping Buddy and Gramps in the fields. She'd grown up with very little knowledge of domesticity.

Her first two attempts were disasters, and she couldn't afford to waste any more flour or yeast. She looked through more cookbooks and found one that explained the processes of kneading, rising, and baking, and what happened during each stage. Once she understood the *why* of baking, the *how* of it fell into place. She tried again and pulled two golden loaves out of the oven. The aroma was overpowering. Mae cut off a thick slab and slathered it with the last of her butter. She closed her eyes and took a bite. Instantly she was surrounded by Gram and Oma working in the kitchen, Gram slicing up bread and Oma putting out a platter of cold chicken and pickles; Gramps and Buddy as they came in from the fields; Mae herself setting the lunch table; and the laughter of an afternoon. The scene was as real to Mae as the delicious sweet heaven that was melting in her mouth.

On Saturday morning, Mae sat at the kitchen table with her first cup of tea. Mastering the baking of bread had buoyed her. Now she needed to really figure out what food she had left and what she had to stock up on.

Yeast. She'd need a jar, if she could get it, or at least several packets.

Flour. There was enough left for two more loaves. Maybe she should get ten more pounds. No, she'd be on the bike. Better get five.

Rice. Dried beans. Tea. Bananas! She craved bananas.

Honey. Could she afford it? Maybe not. Sugar instead. Five pounds.

Butter. Maybe can't afford that either. See how much money is left at the end.

The dandelion greens and leeks from the farm were working great for salad, but maybe add carrots. Carrots sounded wonderful.

Toilet paper. She had two rolls left. Even carefully rationed out, they would eventually be gone. There were stories on the radio about people hoarding toilet paper and stores unable to keep up with demand. What would happen when she ran out?

I could use leaves, I guess.

Mae finished her list and tried to estimate the cost. She counted out some cash and sighed at the dwindling stack of bills.

In the barn she found an old plastic milk crate full of tools. She emptied it out on the workbench, found some twine, and lashed the crate to the rack behind the seat of the bike. She stuck her mask in her pocket, pulled on her helmet, and started down the driveway.

A half hour later Mae was in Welby. Most of the handful of stores along the little main street were empty. They'd recently shut down, she suspected, because of COVID, meaning that people in town had lost jobs because of it. Jobs they really needed. Even if Mae had wanted to work, she doubted any places were hiring. But she wanted to avoid people as much as possible. She'd get by on her own. She didn't want to get sick.

Mae reached Wardell's Hardware Store, next to the post office and just down from the Kari-Out on Welby's little Main Street.

Wardell's. Old pieces of hardware and various implements hanging from the rafters, dust-covered and awaiting the customer who needed just the right whatever. Shelves full of old drawer handles and beautiful glass doorknobs. Rows and rows of little plastic boxes full of screws and nails and grommets and hooks and all kinds of fasteners. Large coils of rope and chain, ready to be custom cut. Old wooden sleds and toboggans, pool noodles and swim toys, toy shovels and plastic pails next to real shovels and metal pails and hoes and rakes. Horse halters and dog food bowls and a ready-to-go aquarium set: "Just add fish." There was barely enough room to walk through the aisles.

Next to the old glass display counter that held the old metal cash register was a rack with just what Mae was looking for: packets of vegetable seeds.

"You'd better get whatcha can now, missy," said the old man without a mask behind the counter. "Folks have been buyin' up seeds for weeks now, and there ain't much left."

"Oh, hi, Mr. Wardell. "It's me, Mae McCain."

"Is that you, Mae? What in the world are you doin' here? Ain't seen you since you was a girl."

"I just moved back to Gramps and Gram's place, and I'm getting the garden back in shape. Um, would you like a mask? I have an extra in my pocket."

"Nah, that's nothin' but a hoax. Somebody made the whole thing up. You can wear one if you want, but I'm not gonna. What the hell happened to yer face?"

Ah. Mae had forgotten about her face. With her mask on, she must look like a pirate or a bank robber from a deal gone bad. No wonder Mr. Wardell hadn't recognized her.

"Just a little accident with the wheelbarrow." She tried to gloss it over, tried to keep the conversation short.

Mae looked at the seed rack. Mr. Wardell was right—it had really been picked over. She wanted to buy her seeds and get out of the store as quickly as possible. She felt uncomfortable being so close to Mr. Wardell. She didn't want to catch his germs or have to listen to his politics.

There was no kale left, but there was Swiss chard. Mae took the last of the remaining seed packets of lettuce, carrots, squash, cucumbers, peas, and green beans. She might not have enough money left for the groceries on her list, but these were more important. They would feed her from late summer into fall.

"You wouldn't believe how many folks've moved up here this spring," said Mr. Wardell as he rang up her seeds. "Every place has been sold or rented. People are plantin' gardens like crazy. Even been askin' me if I sell chicks. *Chicks!* Can you believe it? People are farmin' and gardenin' and they don't even know what the hell they're doin'! And they're all wearin' them stupid masks!"

Mae had to get out of the store. She shoved the money at him and hurried to the door. She breathed deeply when she got outside.

There wasn't much cash left in her pocket. She'd have to prioritize her list.

As it turned out, the convenience store made most of her choices for her. The Kari-Out stocked a few basics and occasionally some honest-to-goodness produce.

Today, no rice, no beans, no yeast, no flour. But yes! Bananas, carrots, and honey. Mae passed on the honey—too expensive—and bought five pounds of sugar instead.

Chester Destry drove out of the valley. The exhaust pipe spewed black smoke into the air as he slowed and turned into the Kari-Out parking lot, which was just about big enough for his truck and the trailer with the massive log skidder perched on top. He hopped down from the truck and jammed a wad of tobacco into his cheek as he walked to the store.

Chester had no social graces or consideration for anyone but himself. He carried a spit can everywhere, even into the Kari-Out for his morning cup of coffee. Customers tended to scatter when he settled into a booth, repelled by both Chester and his brown-stained receptacle.

Today, Mae was the only customer in the store. She'd turned to leave, but the large disheveled man blocked her way.

"Damn, girl," he said as he leered at her. His eyes roved over her body. He smirked as he evaluated the bruises on her face. Drops of brown juice dribbled from the side of his mouth.

"Damn," he said again. "Looks like somebody took care of you pretty good."

Mae was intimidated, then irritated. She pushed past him.

"You're an asshole," she murmured under her breath.

Mae had one more stop to make.

Martina's Bodega was at the end of town. Ernesto Martina

worked as a builder, and Mariella, his wife, ran the little store and restaurant. Mae went in and looked around.

I should have started here, thought Mae. *Rice and beans, of course.*

She also found flour and four packets of yeast.

Mariella stood behind the counter. Her mask was made of colorful Mayan-inspired fabric. After checking out, Mae had just three dollars left.

She hesitated and then asked, "Do you have any tamales?"

One of the best things about Welby on Saturday mornings was Mariella's tamales. If you got there before she sold out.

"I have some, yes," said Mariella.

"How much?" asked Mae.

"Two dollars each."

"Okay, one please. Chicken?"

Mae handed over two dollars and Mariella gave her a large package. When she got to her bike, Mae looked in and saw two tamales. She went back into the store.

"Mariella?" Mae called. "I only paid for one, but you gave me two. I'd buy the second one, but I only have a dollar left."

"Oh, don't worry about it," said Mariella. "I'm almost sold out and business has slowed down. Besides, you look like you could use an extra tamale today."

Once again, Mae had forgotten her face. Not only did she look beat up, but her bike was old and rusty, with a makeshift basket holding her bags. Instantly she was embarrassed about her appearance and what people must think. Mariella saw the shame in Mae's eyes and reached for her hand.

"Look, it's okay. Don't feel bad. Whatever your situation

is, it will get better. You are strong! You will be fine. We all have hard days, sometimes. Come back if you need anything, okay?"

Mae blinked back tears, gratefully thanked Mariella, and walked to her bike. Living on her own, Mae didn't have to think about other people or what they thought of her. Sometimes she forgot to brush her hair or to look in the mirror to see if dirt was smudged across her face. She knew she was strong, and she knew she could live on her own terms. But coming to town had shown her that sometimes other people don't let you do that. They expect you to live on theirs.

Evenings were the hardest. For dinner, Mae usually cooked up a pot of rice and beans, or pasta, or potatoes, and made a salad of foraged greens. Jenny had contributed a few packages of frozen beans and spinach; sometimes Mae mixed those in, too. She'd sit at the table in Gramps's chair and eat in silence, watching the sun dip behind the mountain.

When darkness surrounded the farmhouse, Mae felt truly alone. She'd dial the radio to the local oldies station, wash up the dishes, and then play solitaire with a deck of cards she'd found in a drawer, or work on a book of crossword puzzles someone had gotten for Gram.

Then she'd switch off the radio and move to the living room and read. She'd found books in an upstairs bedroom—books on farming, a few mysteries, and an entire set of the 1950 World Book Encyclopedia.

When Mae turned out the lights and slipped into bed, she fell asleep to silence, broken only by the hoots of an owl and the howls of coyotes. She slept easily.

The phoebe squeaked outside her window. Mae peeked through one eye at the gray morning. With last night's rain the temperature had dropped and the house was cold. She roused out of bed and pulled on her clothes before she started the stove.

Mae was running out of firewood. She'd brought the last of it inside the day after her accident, and it would soon be gone. She'd have to buy more. She got the fire going, then went into the kitchen for a cup of tea. Cup number one.

What would she do today? It depended on the weather. She'd spent the last two days tending to the garden. It had finally warmed up enough to get seeds into the ground, and she'd spent hours raking and hoeing and planting and marking the rows so she could remember what was planted where. She worried about birds eating the seeds, and when they started to grow, would rabbits and woodchucks and deer eat the tender shoots? Should she try to build a fence? How would she do that? She'd need posts and wire fencing, she supposed, and that would use up a lot more of the money she was trying so hard to make last. But she couldn't risk losing her food.

Mae's mood turned sour with her thoughts, and she knew it was because she hadn't been in the woods. There was one part of the farm she still hadn't gotten to, where the property looped over the top and around the back of the mountain, then angled down to the bottom near the western neighbor's pond, then rounded the hill and came out at the driveway. It was a long hike, and she'd have to bushwhack most of it until she reached the pond. From there it was either a long walk down the road or a hard slog through the swamp back to the house. Either way would take a while, but Mae looked forward to it.

She ran to the bathroom to brush her teeth before she left the house. When she opened the medicine cabinet, she saw the box of tampons on the shelf. *One of these days,* she thought, *I'm going to need them.*

And then, the jolt.

How long have I been saying I'm going to need them? Shit! Shitshitshit. Oh, shit!

Mae slid down to the bathroom floor and stared blankly at the wall. Her heart pounded.

Jesus. Oh, Jesus. When was her last period? *Fuck!* It was before she left the city, while she was waitressing. It must have been . . . February. Shit! *Shitshitshit!* Valentine's Day. After they'd closed up the bar, they were already in bed when Max said, "Christ, I forgot to get more condoms. I'm out, babe."

In the heat of the moment, Mae had tried to figure out her last period.

She'd said, "I think I'm okay. I don't think I'm ovulating. Let's just keep going." She'd broken her cardinal rule—condoms every time.

Obviously, she'd miscalculated. Obviously, she'd been ovulating.

Almost three months ago. Why hadn't she realized it when she couldn't eat in the mornings? When her breasts started to feel tender?

Wait, are they tender now? Yeah, a bit. Shit.

With everything that had been going on—the move from the city, losing her cell phone, learning how to live in the country again, the shock of the clear-cut, the accident with the wheelbarrow—she just hadn't paid attention. The one consistent inconvenience in her life that she was supposed to pay attention to, her period, she hadn't, and now *bam!* She was pregnant.

Okay, Mae, think about this. Thinkthinkthink.

All right, two things. First of all, there's no question about keeping it or not keeping it. There's no way I'm going near a doctor or a hospital right now, whether I wanted to or not, so decision is made: keeping it.

Next, Max. Is it imperative for me to tell him right now? No. He left without including me, we were never in love, I don't know where he is other than someplace in Florida, and I have no way of reaching him. Someday maybe I'll have a chance to tell him, but for now, not gonna worry about it.

Another thing: what do I do now? Well, women have been having babies forever. Do I absolutely need medical care? I doubt it. I guess I'll have to make some kind of a plan when the time comes, but for now, pretty sure all I have to do is eat right. Lots of veggies. Lots of protein. I'm glad I still have peanut butter left—I can ask Jenny to pick up some more. And prenatal vitamins. I think I have to drink a lot of water. I bet eggs are really good. I think as long as my body feels good, and I pay close attention, I'm pretty sure I can do this.

Mae felt better after she'd figured that part out. Pregnancy did not have to be a problem if she took care of herself.

Exercise, too, she thought. *Lots of exercise should be*

good for the baby. And me.

The baby. Wow. There was a baby, a little person sprouting inside her. For once in Mae's life, someone else was depending on her. Mae was the only person in the whole world who could take care of this little being inside her.

Holy shit. She was going to be a mother. She started to cry.

Mae rode her bike to the Allen farm. Mrs. Allen let her use the phone again to leave a message for Jenny to please buy her a few things and stop by the house when she could. Mae was grateful that Mrs. Allen had stepped outside and didn't hear "prenatal vitamins" on the list. She didn't want to tell anyone yet except Jenny; she needed time to process her thoughts, to get used to her secret for as long as she could.

As she rode back down the road, two big semis hauling water blasted past her. Now that she was pregnant, it made her think about accidents and protecting the baby. Accidents. Oh, my God—she'd forgotten about her collision with the wheelbarrow and breaking her nose and her black eyes (which, by the way, Mrs. Allen had remarked were looking better).

Could the accident have injured the baby? No, of course not.

Mae realized it was so little and so well protected that she didn't have to worry. She really appreciated her biology classes. And growing up on a farm. She'd witnessed cows getting pregnant and giving birth. For the most part, nature took care of itself.

Mae stopped at the mailbox. Today, a white envelope was inside. It was from Oma.

Mae could barely wait to get to the house to read it. Oma. Oma would be so happy to have a baby in the family again. It would be Oma and Buddy's first great-grandchild! But, wait, would they really be happy?

Mae knew they'd had high hopes that Maggie would go to college, get a good job, probably find a nice guy to marry and settle down with. And then that fell apart. When she was 16, Maggie got pregnant, dropped out of school, and had Mae. Maybe they wouldn't be thrilled after all.

For the first time, Mae thought about how this pregnancy would affect the people she loved. Cyrus would probably be all for it. If Maggie cared one way or the other, she might be happy too. But the family must have had big dreams for Mae not to turn out like Maggie. Mae suddenly felt like she was carrying the weight of Oma and Buddy's pride on her shoulders, and she wondered if she'd once again let them down. First by dropping out of college. Now, with this baby.

A car pulled up to the house. Jenny got out with a whoop and two bags of groceries. She set the bags down on the ground, put on her mask, looked at Mae with delight.

"Pregnant? Pregnant? Oh, my God, Mae! I can't believe it! I am so happy for you! Wait, this is good, right? And what happened to your face?"

"Oh, Jenny. I just realized it this morning. I was so stupid; I should have known it weeks ago. I didn't pay attention."

"Are you happy? Is this good?"

"I think I feel happy and I'm excited and I have so many feelings that I don't even know what they are."

"Is everything okay, Mae? I mean, your body—are you

feeling okay? And what happened to your face?"

"I feel great, I really do! I feel strong and better than I've felt in my life. I guess lots of exercise and no junk food will do that. But when I was moving firewood, my feet slipped out from under me and I hit my face on the wheelbarrow. Or maybe on a piece of wood. Anyway, I think I broke my nose."

All the feelings Mae had been holding in broke loose and she started to sob.

"Oh, no, Mae! Don't cry, honey! Do you want to go to the hospital or a doctor or something?"

"No, thanks." Mae recovered. "I'm okay. It still hurts a little but ice helps. They can't fix a broken nose, and I really don't want to go anywhere near a hospital these days. But thanks."

"If there's anything else you need, just let me know. I got your vitamins and groceries, but if you think of anything else, let me know, okay?"

Mae looked at the grocery receipt. *Damn, prenatal vitamins are expensive!* She put on her mask, stepped closer, and handed Jenny two precious twenty-dollar bills.

"I don't know how to thank you, Jen. I could never do this without your help. You're always coming by and everything. You're such a good friend, and I know I'm going to have lots of questions about pregnancy for you. I just wish I could hug you."

"Me, too, sweetie. I'm so excited for you! I've really gotta run, but I'll see you next week. Oh, here's a present for you." Jenny tossed Mae a roll of toilet paper before she drove away.

Mae went into the house to unpack the groceries, but first she sat down and opened Oma's letter.

Dear Mae,

Thanks for your letters. We are so glad you are on the farm—it would make Gram and Gramps very happy to have the house lived in again.

Things are going okay here. Cyrus is doing his best, and your mother has good days and bad.

Buddy keeps busy with little projects, puttering around, fixing things, and a couple of times a week he goes fishing with the next-door neighbor.

People are really crazy down here. We wear our masks whenever we go to the store, but lots of folks don't—it makes us nervous. So we usually have Cy pick up what we need. I'm so glad you don't have to be around people, honey. I'm really glad you left the city.

Oh, I almost forgot. Check the cellar. There might be some pickles down there that Gram and I had canned up a few years ago. They should still be good.

We all send our love.

Take care, and write again soon, okay?

Love,

Oma

She was wading in the stream, that night, as she slept. The water was cold on her feet but the day was hot and it felt good. The crick was shallow along the sides and she turned over small stones and looked for crayfish and she found one and let its tiny claws pinch her fingers. She looked for the fat little fish that Gramps called stone rollers, and each time she found one she flipped it onto the bank where the cat, waiting, pounced in delight and Mae could hear the cat's jaws crunch the fish bones and the cat was happy. But it was Oma's dream, not Mae's, and somehow Mae was Oma with long blond braids instead of thick brown hair and she was in the middle of the creek and saw a ripple moving fast upstream, coming right at her and the closer it came, the bigger it got and Mae felt alarmed and hopped up onto the top of a rock as the ripple sped past her. She saw that it was an eel and even though she knew it was a fish it startled her because it looked like a snake. Then she was older and there were no more eels and Gramps said it was because the dams stopped them and Mae and Oma were sad and the eels were sad because they could no longer follow their instincts to swim as far upstream as they could possibly go.

After breakfast the next morning, Mae decided to hike. She hadn't been in the woods for three days and she needed to clear her head and sort out her thoughts. She pulled her thick hair back into a ponytail, put a sandwich in her backpack, filled her water bag, and headed up the mountain.

She headed northeast for the first mile and came to the boundary wall. She followed it up and over the top of the mountain till the property line left the wall and cut diagonally through the trees down the back of the mountain, leveling out near the neighbor's pond. The going was tough. In some places she had to pick her way through thick honeysuckle and tree limbs that had dropped in winter storms.

Finally, she rejoined the wall near the bottom of the mountain. Mae was sweating. Gnats bit her arms and flew into her eyes. The day had finally warmed up, and even in the shade of the forest the air felt warm and clammy.

As she made her way through the underbrush, Mae noticed the three red lobes of trillium flowers and patches of yellow trout lilies and their speckled leaves. The forest was springing back to life; Mae thought of the new life that was now part of her. The shock of her pregnancy was lessening. Mae accepted that there would be a baby, that she would be a mother, and that life would soon be very, very different.

Am I happy? Am I excited? I don't know. I really don't know.

Mae crossed through a break in the wall. She didn't see the piece of rusty wire, strung along the base of the opening, that caught the toe of her boot. She went down hard. She had just enough time to put her hands out to keep her face from slamming into the ground.

Oh, fuck! Didn't I just go through this with the wheelbarrow?

She lay still and tried to figure out what hurt.

Head okay. Face okay. Left shoulder sore. Arms sore. Wrists sore. Front okay. Baby? Baby should be okay. Back okay. Both legs seem okay. Left foot okay. Right foot fucking hurts.

Okay, what do I do now? Shitshitshit. Can't lie here. I'll need a crutch. A branch. There's one over there. Reach for it. Farther. Got it.

Now what? I can't slog home through the swamp, that's for sure. Neighbor's pond. Just aim for the neighbor's pond. Shit, it hurts!

Mae heaved herself up from the ground and groaned. She balanced on her left foot, pushed against the branch, and straightened her body. She could hardly bear the pain as she placed the toes of her right foot down, then hopped. She squealed at the sharp jab on the side of her ankle. Her eyes teared up. This was not going to work. She was too far from the house, and there was too much pain.

"Okay, Fifi," she said out loud, "let's try something different."

Mae tentatively tried placing the ball of her foot down first, then put a tiny bit of weight on it. Better. It made her breathe in sharply, but there was less pain when she hopped. Mae slowly made her way along the trail, stopping to sit on a log or boulder every few steps.

Shit, she said to herself. *Is this my punishment for getting pregnant?*

"Shit," she said out loud, "Shitshitshit." The sweat ran down her face, and she felt her shirt sticking to her back. She pushed aside some hair that had fallen across her eyes. She forced herself to a tree stump 20 feet down the path, sat down, and gulped some water.

"Okay," she said aloud, "this trail goes past the pond. If I cut through that field, I can get to the old Hubbard cabin on the next road over. Maybe somebody's there."

The decision did not come lightly. If no one was home, Mae would be at least a quarter mile farther from the farmhouse. But if someone was there and could give her a ride, it would save her hours of hopping. And pain. Lots of pain.

The pond should be just around that jog down the trail.

Mae hoisted herself back up on her good leg and steeled herself against the pain. She started again. Foot down, gasp, hop. Foot down, gasp, hop.

By the time Mae rounded the bend, she was nauseous and drenched in sweat. Fifty feet ahead of her stretched the dark water of the pond. And there, on the far side, was a boy who looked up in surprise as a stranger, a young woman, hobbled out of nowhere and fell to the ground.

CHAPTER SEVEN

Ruth, December 1941

Within a year Ruth had more than 200 flight hours under her belt. She earned her instructor rating, and became Ulster County's first female commercial pilot. Mr. Hasbrough nicknamed her "'the Dawn Patrol," and he offered her a job to help ferry aircraft between his airports in New York and Florida. The strategy allowed his instructing school to operate year 'round. Like migrating birds, his planes headed south in late fall and returned to New York in the spring.

The trip south in December 1941 was off to an unpromising start.

"Can we leave today, Chet?" Ruth asked as she checked in with the other pilot who was also waiting to transport one of Hasbrough's planes south. After four days of delay, the exasperation in Ruth's voice pierced the phone. It was critical to get the planes out of New York before winter weather moved in, yet here they were, stuck in a pattern of rain, fog, and drizzle. Ruth absentmindedly fingered the coin in her pocket, knowing the answer before she'd even asked.

"Not today, Ruth." Chet sounded weary and defeated. "I've got hourly weather reports coming in, but today's a washout. Call me again in the morning."

The cloud cover was basically at ground level. Day after

day, the weather had socked them in. Each morning, Ruth had made the call and gotten the same answer. Finally, on the morning of December 6, the clouds broke. Ruth and Chet were on their way.

The two planes stopped in Lancaster, Pennsylvania, to refuel with no time to spare. They touched down on the Washington, DC airstrip just before dusk. Supper was a sandwich at a nearby diner, and they were in their rooms for an early lights-out. To reach the airport at Sanford, Florida, by the following evening, they had to be up and away at first light.

The next morning was sunny and clear with some high, light clouds in the sky. Perfect flying weather. The two pilots completed their preflight checklists, taxied to the runway, and took off on a southerly heading. With a slight tailwind, the planes flew a straight course and by late afternoon were within sight of Savannah, Georgia.

Suddenly, two army aircraft appeared alongside each plane. The young pilot to Ruth's right seemed distressed and was gesticulating enthusiastically. He pointed at Ruth, then the ground, then back at Ruth, and then back at the ground. He also appeared to be yelling, but she obviously couldn't hear him and his excitement kept her from being able to read his lips or guess his meaning. Since the pilot off her other wing was signaling just as passionately and with even greater agitation, Ruth decided she should probably head toward the ground. The flailing aviators struck her as kind of comical and ridiculous, but she suppressed an urge to smile. Whatever was going on had to be serious. She cut her speed and aimed for the Savannah airfield. As the two escorts guided her to the runway and into the administration building, Ruth saw that Chet had been ushered in with two chaperones of his own.

"What the HELL are you doing IN THE AIR?" demanded an army officer. "Don't you know that ALL PRIVATE AIRCRAFT have been GROUNDED?" The officer slammed his fist onto his desk. He looked at Chet, then at Ruth, then at Chet again in total exasperation.

"Ah, permission to speak, sir?" asked Chet, not sure if, as a civilian, he already had permission to speak, could ask for permission to speak, or was simply supposed to speak.

"WHAT?" bellowed the officer.

"Sir," said Chet, "we took off at seven-thirty this morning from Washington, DC. At that time, there was no directive to keep private aircraft grounded. We need to get these planes to Florida. Respectfully speaking, what the hell is going on, sir?"

The officer took a breath. He looked exhausted.

"We will do our best to get your paperwork cleared and get you on your way," came the reply. "At thirteen-thirty this afternoon, the Japanese executed an air attack on our base at Pearl Harbor, Hawaii. We are about to go to war."

CHAPTER EIGHT

Wesley, April 2020

Wesley didn't know what to do. Should he run home? Jack bounded to the other side of the pond and wagged his tail as he sniffed at the person. Better follow Jack and go over there. Wesley walked toward the woman on the ground. He sidled up slowly, suspicious of the situation. The woman had black and blue bruises around her eyes and cuts on her swollen nose. She was crying, but she was also half-laughing at Jack's soft tongue as he licked the tears from her face.

Mae looked up at the boy who stood back, hesitant and silent. He seemed to be afraid of her.

"Hi, there," she said. "I'm really sorry if I frightened you. I know I look scary. I hit my face with a wheelbarrow. My foot is hurt and I can't walk on it."

He gaped at her, eyes bigger than before. Nothing she said made any sense.

Mae noticed that one of the boy's eyes was kind of crossed and looked downward toward his nose.

Mae asked, "Does your dog have a name?"

"Umm. J-Jack."

"Pleased to meet you, Mr. Jack," she said, stroking the dog's long, soft hair.

"What's your name?" she asked the boy.

He gave a wary look.

"W-W-Wesley," he finally answered. My name is Wesley

C-Carter."

"Well, Mr. Carter," Mae said, grimacing as she sat up, "it's nice to meet you. My name is Mae McCain, and I am in a little trouble, as you can see. You don't by any chance live in that cabin across the field, do you?"

"Y-yep," said Wesley. "M-m-me and my dad live there. D-do you think I should go get him?"

"That would be great, Wesley. Maybe if he has a truck or something, he could drive me home."

Wesley ran fast across the field with Jack at his heels. This was important. Someone needed his help, and for the first time in his life, Wesley felt a sense of responsibility swell inside his chest.

Mae scooted to the edge of the pond, removed her boot, and slipped her ankle into the cold water. Instant relief. Ten minutes later, a banged-up pickup truck cut across the field and maneuvered close to the pond. A skinny guy jumped out and crossed over to her.

"Hey, there! Wesley says you got hurt. Let's take a look."

Mae slowly eased her leg out of the water. The man knelt down and took her foot. His hands felt rough, but they were gentle. His clothes were worn and he smelled like sawdust. Bits of it clung to his sweatshirt.

"I was hiking and I tripped on some wire. I think I sprained it."

"You've got some pretty good swelling going on. It's going to be colorful in a few days; it'll match your face." He smiled at her. "Uh, by the way, you look like crap. I hope the other guy looks worse."

He concentrated on her ankle. "I brought an ACE bandage; okay if I wrap it up?"

"Yeah, oh, thank you," said Mae. "You seem to know your way around an injured foot."

"Kind of have to. Living this far out, there's not much choice but to self-treat everything that doesn't kill you. My name is Jimmy Carter, by the way."

"Really? Jimmy Carter?" Even with the pain, Mae couldn't help but grin at him.

"I know. Go ahead and laugh. I thought I'd get it over with. I usually go by James. Wesley and I are renting the old Hubbard place."

"Nice to meet you, James. I'm Mae McCain. I'm staying at the Griffin farm. Can you give me a lift back home?"

"No problem. We'll get you home." James helped Mae to her feet.

She still felt weak, but between the cool water and the bandage, Mae definitely felt better. James helped her to the pickup and boosted her into the passenger seat.

Jack and Wesley were waiting in the back seat. James turned the key. The engine turned over, but didn't start. After two more tries, the truck spit and sputtered and finally started. James turned around and raised his hand. He and Wesley high-fived, and the truck slowly made its way back through the field and out to the road.

Mae didn't have her mask or any spares with her.

Damn, she thought, *I need to keep some masks in my backpack.*

She rolled down her window as far as it would go and breathed in the outside air. James had his window down, too; she hoped it would be enough to keep them all from getting COVID.

Wesley liked seeing Mae in the front seat with his dad. It made his heart feel warm and full. A smile pulled at the corners of his mouth. He'd done good, and he felt proud. And no one had ever called him "Mr. Carter" before.

CHAPTER NINE
Mae, May 2020

Two weeks later, the battered old pickup truck pulled into the driveway just as Mae finished her lunch. She was sitting outside, her ankle bandaged and propped up on the edge of the wheelbarrow. Her backpack, with everything she thought she might need, was on the ground beside her.

James, Wesley, and Jack all piled out of the driver's side door. Jack raced over to slobber a hello on Mae's face, while Wesley followed close behind. "How's the ankle?" James asked. "Just push Jack away, Mae—he gets way too enthusiastic."

"Oh, he's fine! I haven't been kissed like that in a long time." Mae reddened when she realized what she'd said. "Um, I mean, I didn't mean it like it sounded. Oh, gosh, I'm— Aargh!"

James grinned.

"Right. Anyway, I've been hobbling more and more every day," she said. "It doesn't hurt if I don't overdo it. I think it could have been a lot worse."

"Oh, good. Hey, if you don't mind I'd like to ask you a favor. My friend Casey was supposed to pick up a load of wood, but his truck broke down. I was wondering if Wes and Jack could stay with you for a few hours while I deliver it to him. I should be back before dinner."

Wesley was kind of hopping up and down, and Mae could

see he was really hoping she'd say yes.

"Well, Wesley," Mae said, "I looked at my calendar this morning, and the only thing it said was to play with you this afternoon."

Wesley's eyes grew wide and his face opened into a big grin. He turned and looked at his father.

"Sh-she said yes, Dad! She said yes!"

"Oh, thanks a lot Mae," James said with relief. "Wesley, you behave yourself, you hear? I'll be back as soon as I can."

With that, James was in the truck and down the driveway.

"Well, what would you like to do, Wesley?" asked Mae.

"I dunno. What is there?"

"Let's think. It's not too cold, so I'd like to stay outside. I can't go very far, but we could do a little exploring and see what we can find. Sound okay to you?"

"Yes!" said Wesley. He helped Mae stand up and looked very concerned as she got her balance.

"A-are you sure you're okay?" he asked anxiously. "We don't have to go."

"Oh, don't you worry about me, Mr. Carter! I'm almost ready. I just need Buddy's old crutches. Can you please hand them to me?"

Wesley watched carefully as Mae adjusted them under her arms.

"All right, let's go! Oh, wait a second, Wesley." Mae reached into her backpack for her mask. Then she pulled out a smaller one she'd made the night before. It was black, with a red lightning bolt. "Hey, Wesley, do you mind wearing this?"

"W-what is it?"

"It's a special protection mask. When we wear them, they'll keep us safe, okay? We can make believe we're robbers."

"COOL!" yelled Wesley. He slipped his on and ran ahead with Jack.

Mae made her way slowly behind them.

The three of them headed into the pasture. Jack raced out in front, then raced back. Then raced ahead again, then raced back. He clearly enjoyed being on an adventure with his boy and their new friend.

Wesley didn't leave Mae's side. Walking next to her, he felt the swell of responsibility again, just like when he'd rescued her. He felt it was his duty to keep an eye on her and guard her.

"A-are you sure you're okay? D-do you want to sit down?" he asked.

"Aw, thanks, Wesley. I'm fine. But I bet I'll be ready to sit when we get to that stone wall."

They reached it and Wesley clambered up to sit next to Mae.

"Tell me, Wesley, what do you see?"

"I see the field on that side, and the field on this side. And the wall we're on."

"What else?"

"I see trees, and grass, and the sky."

"Is anybody in the trees?"

"Um. I see a crow. And I think a squirrel. And look! There's a chipmunk looking at us from those rocks!"

"Good job, buddy! Very observant!"

"Ahserfent," said Wesley. "What's ahserfent?"

"OB-SER-VANT," said Mae. "It means you're good at paying attention."

"Well, my teacher never told me that. She said I don't never pay attention."

Mae looked at Wesley and thought.

"How old are you, Wesley? What grade are you in?"

"I am six years old. I am in first grade," he said proudly.

"Why aren't you in school today?"

"COVID. We can't go to school 'cuz of COVID."

"Well, doesn't your teacher teach you online?"

"I don't think so."

Mae was concerned.

"Do you have classes at your house on a computer?"

"No." He seemed sad.

"Why not, Wesley?"

Tears came to his eyes. "'Cuz I don't have a c-capooter."

Mae's heart fell, and her eyes teared up, too. She cleared her throat.

"Well, then, Mr. Carter," she declared with determination. "Since you don't have a computer, we'll just have our own classes."

Mae and Wesley talked about the clouds, and what makes them. They talked about the mice that live in the fields, what they eat, and what eats them. They talked about the stone wall they were sitting on. How long ago was it built, and who built it?

They started back toward the house. Jack was busy sniffing around a clump of grass, and Wesley was still glued to Mae's side. She stopped to rest on an old tree stump and looked down at a nearby anthill.

"Wesley," Mae said, "do you know the alphabet?"

"The what?" he asked.

"Um. The ABCs. Do you know your ABCs?"

"Oh, yes! I can sing the song!"

And he broke into "ABCDEahG. HIJK emma nemmo P. umaREST. TUVdoubleleeS. Wisey. Now I know my ABCs. Tell me whatchu think a me."

"Well done, Wesley!" Mae said. "What does A stand for?"

"A is for APPLE!" Wesley yelled.

"Great!" said Mae. "What else?"

"Nothing," said Wesley.

Mae was surprised. "Why not?" she asked.

"The apple is the only picture in the book," he said.

"Oh, I see. Okay. Then that's where we'll start."

Mae wrote A in the dirt with a twig. She handed it to Wesley. He wrote a crooked A, but an A, nonetheless.

"Now," said Mae, "I want you to poke the stick into that little hill."

Wesley jammed it into the sandy mound and prodded. He pulled it out and jabbed it back in.

"Now let's watch," she said. "Let's see what happens."

In moments, a mob of ants spilled out onto the dirt.

"Ants!" yelled Wesley, enthusiastically. "Lots and lots of ants!"

"Right!" yelled Mae. "And what does ANT start with?"

Wesley looked at her blankly.

"A!" she yelled.

"A!" he yelled.

Jack left the grass clump and bolted over to join in the excitement. He jumped on Wesley, who fell down in the grass, laughing. Jack climbed up on the stump and kissed Mae's face.

School had begun.

James's truck sputtered to a stop in the driveway. By the time Mae and Wesley got outside, James had piled a stack of wood by the barn.

"Nights can still get cold around here, Mae, even in the summer. Thought you might need this. And thanks for watching Wesley for me."

Mae remembered how Gram had often gone to the attic for extra blankets during months that were supposed to be warm, when the stove was out. There were pictures of Mae and Gary bundled up the summer when they were little, when the temperature barely reached into the sixties and the sun didn't want to shine. And Gramps had said that over his lifetime in the Catskills he'd seen snow during every month of the year.

Mae thanked James for the wood and said it was fun playing with Wesley and Jack. She wasn't sure if James was one of the people against masking up, and she didn't want to offend him, but now, especially now that she knew she was pregnant, she needed him to wear one. She'd seen his look of surprise when he saw the little mask on Wesley's face, and she took a deep breath. Hesitantly she asked if he would wear the mask she held out to him.

"Oh, please, Dad, please!" yelled Wesley. "Then we can

be robbers together!"

"Oh, okay, Wes," he said. "I know it's important to some people, Mae, and I'm not sure what I think yet, but yes, I will wear it when I see you." He slid on the mask, a larger version of Wesley's.

"Cool, Dad! Look at us!"

As Wesley and Jack climbed into the truck, James turned to Mae.

"I haven't seen Wesley this excited about anything in a long time. He seems to really like being with you, Mae. I just want to thank you."

"I really like being with him, too. And I'm happy to watch him anytime. It's not like I have a lot to do around here."

James got in. The truck coughed twice, then started and headed down the driveway.

Two days later, Mae sat at the kitchen table, morning tea in hand. She picked up Oma's letter and read it again. She'd forgotten about the cellar. Her food supply would increase if there were still jars of pickles down there.

She pulled on a sweater, gently laced up her hiking boots, and went outside. The hinges of the rusted cellar doors creaked as Mae hefted one side up and propped it open. The narrow concrete steps were steep and crumbling. She was in darkness at the bottom and just in time remembered the shallow drainage pit, stepped over it, then reached up and gave the bare bulb a turn. The light flickered on. Mae hadn't been down there for years. The little red tricycle that had first been Maggie's, then Mae's, stood in the middle of the room as though it knew the next generation was on its way. Leaning against a corner was the fishing pole she'd used as a girl. Old boards and paint cans were stacked against one wall.

To her right were the shelves that held rows of dusty canning jars. Mae limped toward them, hoping at least some of them were full. She wasn't disappointed. There were jars of beets, green beans, tomato sauce. Yellow squash. Pumpkin. Rhubarb. Peppers, carrots, and leeks. And jams! Jars and jars of strawberry, blueberry, and blackberry jam. Some jars were labeled in Oma's careful handwriting and some in Gram's shakier scrawl. Mae pressed down on the tops and breathed a sigh of relief—the lids were tight. The pickles and preserves were still good. Now she had enough food to last until the garden began to produce.

She took as many jars as she could hold, grabbed the fishing pole, and turned out the lightbulb. She hobbled gingerly up the steps.

It felt like Christmas as she wiped dust from the jars and placed them on the kitchen shelves. She smeared a slice of bread with strawberry jam and closed her eyes while the sweetness whirled through her mouth to her brain. There was strength in that little jar; Gram and Oma had filled it with love, and once more Mae knew she was where she belonged.

CHAPTER TEN

Ruth, May 1943

Dear Mom,

I can hardly believe I have time to write. Even though six months of basic training is almost over, they keep us busy from dawn till dinner, and then we study until 10, when I can hardly keep my eyes open. Before I know it, my alarm goes off at 6 and I start all over again. I roll out of my bunk and wash up and dress. Then I grab my bugle so I can be at the flagpole by 7 to play reveille. Then there's an hour of calisthenics (which I'm very good at, by the way), and then breakfast and off to classes.

It's been inconvenient to live off-base. Most of the time we have a ride to our rooms; there's a fellow named Frank who drives the truck to ferry us back and forth morning and night. But sometimes some of us get delayed, you know, and then we're stuck and need to get a cab if we can split it, or just start walking. The next class will have it easier in Sweetwater; the barracks will be right on the base. Those girls won't know how lucky they are to roll out of bed an hour later than we do!

Anyway, we just found out that we'll be ferrying all the planes across Texas from here at Houston over to Sweetwater right before graduation. We can't wait—it'll be our first mission!! After graduation we'll be flying everyday, picking planes up at factories and flying them to air bases where the men will take them overseas. We can't wait!

Our days are jam-packed, Mom, with lessons until noon and flight time whenever we can get it. We all know how to fly, of course, but the instructors just drill, drill, drill facts and charts and flight plans and diagrams and math calculations into our heads.

We have two main instructors—Wilson is quite a bit older than we are, and quite nice to us. The other one, Burger, might be in his 20s, like most of us, and boy, is he difficult. I think he resents "wasting" his time and energy on us because we're girls, and he doesn't make it easy for us. He makes some of the gals cry—they try to blink back their tears until he's gone—but Wilson says not to pay any attention to Burger. Just learn what he teaches us and forget him.

We'll get more air time between now and next month when we graduate. That's the fun part. These military planes are something else. And we'll get to fly them across Texas!

Mom, remember I mentioned Martha in

my last letter? We bunk next to each other and we get along like sisters. It's so much easier to have someone to eat with and study and share clothes with if we don't have a chance to get our laundry done.

We're thinking that after graduation we'll take the train together, and I'll stop off in Pennsylvania with her for a couple of days before I come home.

And what do you hear from Doug? Is my big brother coming home on leave anytime soon? It would be swell if we could all be there at the same time.

Give my love to Pop, and whoever else is home. I miss you all very much, but Mom, believe me that being part of this flying group is the most exciting thing I've ever done in my life!

Can't wait to see you,
Ruth

CHAPTER ELEVEN
Wesley, May 2020

Wesley and Jack wandered through the field to the pond. Mae was usually there after breakfast. Wesley couldn't wait to see her. Mae was so much fun, and she was nice. They had adventures, and she played with him, and her face looked better, too.

Wesley saw that Mae was waiting for him. He pulled his robber mask out of his pocket and put it on.

"My dad says I don't have to wear it at home," he said.

"He's right, Wesley, just when you're with people you don't live with."

"Okay," he said as he picked up a stick and threw it into the pond.

"What shall we do today?" asked Mae. "Do you want to go to the swamp or through the woods?"

"Woods!" yelled Wesley. Jack tore ahead with Mae and Wesley following behind. Her ankle was just about healed and she could almost keep up with them.

They found a clearing partway up the mountain trail that was covered in a thick green ground cover.

"Lycopodia!" yelled Mae. "Look, Wesley! L is for *Lycopodia*!"

"Lycompondia!" yelled Wesley.

They dropped down on the ground and looked at the plants.

"See its yellow hat? This kind is called *Lycopodia obscuratum*. And look—here's some *complanatum*!" Mae searched around some more and found what she was looking for.

"But, Wesley, this is my favorite! *Lycopodia lucidulum*! That means bright and shiny! See how pretty it is?"

Mae and Wesley jumped up and down yelling "*Lycopodia lucidulum*!" while Jack bounced up and down beside them.

Mae told Wesley how she and Gram and Oma used to gather the plants just after Thanksgiving and weave them into Christmas wreaths, then decorate them with red bows.

"When you pick them, Wesley, only pick a few from one place, then move on and pick more from another place. Keep moving through the patch, and make sure you leave more than you take. That way, there will always be some for next time, okay?"

"Okay, Mae!" he said. He was a willing student and very eager to please.

"Hey, Wesley, can I ask you something?"

"Sure."

"Um, does the doctor know about your eye?"

Wesley looked a little embarrassed.

"This one?"

"Yep."

"Yep. I seen him about it."

"What did he say?"

"I don't know. I don't remember."

"Well, did he give you a patch to wear on the other one? To help make this one stronger?"

"Yeah, he did. But I don't wear it."

"How come, Wes?"

Wesley teared up.

"Because it looks funny. Kids at school made fun of me. They laughed at me, and I felt bad so I took it off and I never worn it again."

Mae hugged him.

"Oh, Wesley, I'm sorry." She hugged him tighter.

Wesley hadn't been hugged like that in a long time. His dad would put his arms around Wesley to pick him up, or would put a hand on his shoulder, and of course hugged him and gave him a kiss at bedtime. His teachers had always given little hugs to all the kids. But this was a real hug, big and full and tight. It was like maybe his mom would have hugged him. Wesley felt a pull on his heart he hadn't felt before, that was full and good, but sad. He melted into Mae and sobbed.

"Oh, sweetie," Mae said. She felt helpless. She didn't know what else to do but keep hugging him. She wanted to ask about his mother. This little boy had a dad who obviously loved him, but there was still a void in his life. She didn't dare ask; she didn't know how or even if she should.

After a while, Wesley pulled his head away and stopped sniffling. Mae wiped his face with her shirt.

"Hey, Wesley. Would you do me a favor? Would you please wear your eye patch again? You don't even see those kids now, and I would like to see how it looks on you. I think it would make you look like a pirate!"

"A pirate! A robber pirate!" yelled Wesley. "I could wear my mask and my patch and I would be a robber pirate!"

"Aargh! Aye, Pirate Wesley!" yelled Mae.

CHAPTER TWELVE

Mae, June 2020

Mae was fifteen and shooting baskets. The hoop was attached to the side of the barn and she bounced the basketball on the road because no cars ever, hardly ever, came past and she and Gary could play H-O-R-S-E for an hour without having to stop and move out of the way. But this night she was shooting baskets by herself and as the sun went down the bats started flying from the barn, hundreds of them, swirling above the road and the stream, catching mosquitoes, and sometimes she heard little squeaks if they flew close to her head. She imagined she was one of them flying and squeaking in the setting sun and she stopped shooting baskets so she could watch their crazy flight, hundreds of bats swooping in all directions, and she didn't know why they didn't crash into each other or into her or the barn, but she thought they must be very smart and she loved them.

The sounds of the birds woke Mae, but before she opened her eyes, she smelled the change in the air. Spring, what she thought of as real spring, not the muddy, chilly beginning, but the part when the trees leafed out and blooms began to pop, was finally here. The first week in June was the best-smelling week of the year. Gram's rows of lilacs bent over the driveway, heavy with blooms. The perfume nearly intoxicated Mae as she walked to the mailbox. No letter from Oma today, but today Mae felt that nothing could get her down.

Back at the house, Mae noticed the fishing pole she'd brought up from the cellar, standing in the corner of the mudroom and waiting to be used. The reel still worked, and there was a rusty, barbed hook on the line.

She could dig worms in the loosened soil of the garden. The stream beside the house had a few pools deep enough to have sizable fish—eight or nine inches long, enough meat on them to make a meal. She hadn't had trout for years. Gramps and Buddy would bring home their catch, cleaned and ready for Gram or Oma to dredge in flour and fry up with butter, just a few short minutes on each side. Mae remembered when she was little, crunching on the crispy tail while Oma gently pulled the spine away from the body, saying to *always* remove all, *all* of the bones or they might catch in her throat and she could die. After carefully confirming there were no bones, Mae was finally allowed to eat the soft and flaky meat, gamey but wonderful, almost melting in her mouth.

Mae had been fishing since she could remember. It wasn't hard at all. Just bait the hook and wait for a fish to take the worm. But killing the fish was tougher. She'd have to use her hands, or a rock, or a knife . . . she didn't use to mind it. But could she do it now? Did she want to?

Not today. How about this, Fifi? If I start to crave it, I'll do it. I'll do anything for the baby. But till then, I'll rely on peanut butter and eggs for protein and hope that's enough.

Mae placed the fishing pole back in the corner and headed out for a hike.

The fields and woods that morning were filled with scents of honeysuckle and apple blossoms. Even the ripening grasses sweetened the air. Vibrant pinkster bushes punctuated the old logging roads, and Mae plunged her nose into the rose-colored flowers and inhaled the most luscious of the mountain's scents. *Is this why the bees do it?* she wondered. *Are they as captivated by the smell as I am?* The aromas pulled her back into childhood.

Mae kept an eye out for the strange-looking lady slippers that sometimes dotted the ground under the trees. Buddy had called their erotic, wrinkled plum shapes "testicle flowers," which elicited giggles from Mae and Gary and Gram, but exasperated eye-rolls from Oma.

Mae hiked higher on the mountain, then suddenly stopped. There it was—she heard it again faintly, barely loud enough to make out. Mae held her breath, willing it to sound again. Then, louder this time, back in the trees to her right, the ethereal notes of a hermit thrush wafted through the air and into her body, as intoxicating as any substance she'd ever imbibed or inhaled, and she closed her eyes and soared. She hadn't heard the song since she'd left for college a half-dozen years before. But for most of her teenage years, it had saved her. When she'd run to the woods on those dark days when she'd not known how to center herself, before she ever knew herself, the thrush's fluting song had struck her soul so deeply that it buoyed her, lifted her enough that she could return to the farmhouse and reconnect, rejoin the family she loved. And now, after so many years, the song filled her again. Elated her, settled her, centered her.

Moments later, the singing stopped. Mae opened her eyes,

inhaled deeply, and headed back to the house.

The farm had been the perfect place for Mae to do much of her growing up. If she had a choice, it could be the perfect place to raise her child. But how would she be able to do that? With Gram and Gramps gone, Oma and Buddy would probably have to sell the farm.

No use thinking about that now, Fifi, she told herself. *Let's just get through having this baby. One thing at a time.*

CHAPTER THIRTEEN
Ruth, June 1943

"What do you mean we can't take off? We've been sitting here since yesterday!" Ruth and the other pilots were livid. They'd arrived in Tulsa, Oklahoma, three days before to pick up and deliver ten P-51s to the east coast. No one could tell them anything except they were grounded until further notice. They spent rest of the day trying to stave off boredom: playing cards, sunbathing in a hidden corner behind the barracks, rolling dice. The rim of the silver dollar Ruth kept in her pocket was beaten and dented from hours of being bounced on the ground, usually when her flights were socked in by bad weather. Today she ricocheted it off the sidewalk in the bright sunshine, cursing the waste of good weather.

Ruth had always been confident, but the dollar in her pocket gave her an extra edge of assurance. The silver dollar girl even felt like company when Ruth was by herself. The women waited out the day. When the sun rose the next morning, they were finally given the go-ahead to fly.

Ruth was first in the string of Mustangs ready to leave. She taxied onto the runway and revved the engine. With the throttle pushed forward, the plane roared and picked up speed. It lifted from the ground and started to gain altitude. Ruth reached for the lever to up-lock the landing gear, and, abruptly, the engine died. She knew there was no reasonable explanation for the P-51 to quit. Traveling at more than 150 miles an hour, Ruth was headed directly toward an administration building, two gas trucks, and a crowd at the end of the runway.

Dear God, she thought, *let this end well.*

Her extensive training kicked into action. She forced the nose down and set the plane back on the runway. She heard the screech of the disintegrating tires as she watched the crowd scatter in front of her. Just before reaching the fuel trucks, the plane came to a halt.

Ruth calmly climbed out of the cockpit. The tires had been worn down to their hubs, and she breathed a sigh of relief that she hadn't been able to lift them. As she joined her friends, who had left their planes and gathered at the edge of the tarmac, Ruth reached into her pocket and rubbed the face of the girl on the silver dollar.

Ruth's training, composure, and quick thinking had probably saved her life, and those of the crew on the ground. Almost certainly the aborted flight had saved the lives of at least some of the nine other women waiting to take off. Later they found out that water had infiltrated the airfield's underground fuel storage tanks. All the planes' tanks had to be drained before they could be refueled. Was that the reason they'd been grounded for four days? Why had the women's planes still held contaminated fuel?

"I thought you were a goner, Ruthie," said Martha, as they climbed onto their cots that night. "I don't know what I would have done without you."

"Well, you'd have carried on," Ruth told her. "You'd have been sad, but then you'd have to just climb into a plane and keep flying."

"You know what," Ruth continued, "that would actually be the best thing you could ever do. If anything does happen to me, I want you to get up into the sky as soon as possible, because then you'll be flying for both of us."

"Deal," said Martha.

"Deal," said Ruth.

They turned out the light and went to sleep.

CHAPTER FOURTEEN

Wesley, June 2020

Some days when the air currents were just right, the sound of the bottle machine wafted up the valley from the water plant toward Wesley's house. The machine pressing down into the plastic went *thump thump thump* like the footfalls of a giant stomping across the fields. Then, as it lifted upward from the plastic form, the hydraulic mechanism forced air back into the equipment and caused a *whoosh whoosh whoosh* like the breath of a monster that reverberated off the mountain and across the valley.

Yesterday's air currents were different and Wesley couldn't hear the monster. He figured it was sleeping, or breathing so quietly that he couldn't tell where it was, so he almost forgot about it and spent the day chasing frogs with Jack. But today the enormous gasps returned, and Wesley's heart beat faster. The fear welled up once again within him. He ran to the secluded fort he'd made in the trees behind his house, with Jack close on his heels.

Once inside, hidden from the giant, Wesley felt a little safer. He sat down on the ground and reached behind his stockpile of stones to dig out the sharp hunting knife he'd taken from his dad's dresser. He'd felt bad about taking it, but he needed to sharpen the large spears that his dull little penknife couldn't hone. His dad would get real mad if he knew Wesley had swiped the knife, and Wesley couldn't tell him. Nobody could find out about his fort or his weapons. Ever. They had to stay secret.

Working to build his little arsenal relieved some of Wesley's anxiety. As he whittled a branch down to a sharp point, he thought of his dad and Jack and Mae and how he would fight the monster to protect them.

I should have more stone piles in the woods, he thought. *I could hide spears behind trees along the trails. I'll hide apples for food and blankets to sleep on. If he's as big as he sounds, I can run faster than he can and I'll hide in the ledges and behind trees. I could get him to follow me up the mountain while Dad and Mae and Jack escape. Then I'll start a rockslide that will push him off the top. When I come home, everyone will be there and they'll be so happy that I killed the giant. We'll all be safe.*

I wanted to see Mae today, he thought. *But this is more important. I'll see her tomorrow.*

The next day, Mae waited again near the pond for Wesley. He didn't always show up, but then neither did she. They had an informal arrangement and gave each other ten or 15 minutes before going on. Mae was about to leave when she saw Jack and Wesley racing across the field.

"Ahoy, Mae!" shouted Wesley as he came to a stop, trying to catch his breath. He was wearing his mask and his eye patch.

"Aargh, Pirate Wesley! You won't be robbin' me today, will ye?"

Mae hugged him and he squealed with delight.

"Dad burned the eggs this morning and had to make breakfast all over again! I was afraid you'd be gone!"

"Oh, no, Wes, I figured you'd be coming! Hey, there, Jack! How are you today, boy?" Mae bent down to pet him. She received sloppy kisses in return.

"Look what I've got, Wesley!"

Mae moved aside to show him her backpack, a rolled-up tent, and a bedroll.

"What's that for?"

"Camping. I'm going to sleep out tonight."

"Why?" asked Wesley. "Won't you be scared?"

"Nah!" said Mae, "There's nothing to be scared of. I used to camp out with my cousin when we weren't much older than you. Come on, you can help me pitch my tent."

They headed up the mountain. Jack constantly ran ahead, then doubled back. They hiked along the wall to the ledges and scrambled among the rocks. The spaces between the boulders were large enough for Wesley to squeeze into; one was large enough for Mae as well. Jack whined and squirmed through the hole until he was sitting on Mae's lap. Wesley squealed with laughter as Jack leaned back into Mae and thoroughly washed her face with his tongue.

"Ugh! Ugh! Dog germs!" Mae yelled, as she pushed Jack out of the hole and crawled back outside. Wesley tumbled out behind her, and they continued up the mountain.

Mae chose a spot for her tent between the ledges and a small pond.

"Look at this, Wesley; this is called a vernal pool."

"Vernan pool," said Wesley.

"Ver-nal. Ver-nal," said Mae. "A vernal pool is a small pocket of water that's only here in the woods in the springtime. It collects water from when the snow melts and when it rains. Animals and birds drink the water, and frogs lay their eggs here, see?"

Mae pointed out the clumps of jelly-like eggs.

"Cool!" said Wesley. "Maybe when they hatch, Jack and I can come back and catch them!"

"Yep, maybe!" said Mae.

She unrolled her bundles and began to pitch her tent. It hadn't been used since she and Gary were teenagers. Pitching it reminded her of how much fun she'd had growing up on the farm. They had camped in this same spot, cooking hot dogs over a fire and drinking bottles of Buddy's beer that they'd snuck out of the house.

"Oh, shite!" Mae said out loud. "I forgot the stakes."

"Shite?" asked Wesley. "What does that mean?"

"Oh, shite," she said again. "I shouldn't have said that."

"What does it mean?" Wesley asked again.

"It's Irish," said Mae. "It's a swear word, kind of."

"Can I say it?" asked Wesley.

"Well, sometimes," said Mae. "Other times you can say merde."

"Mard!" said Wesley.

"No, MERDE. It's French."

"It's okay to say them?"

"Sometimes," said Mae. "But not too much."

"But what do they mean?"

"I don't want to tell you."

"Then how will I know when to say them?"

"Just don't say them very often and you won't get into

trouble. Most people don't know what they mean."

"Okay, Mae."

Mae fastened the tent ropes around rocks to secure the sides. The center pole held the tent high enough that she could get in. She unrolled her sleeping bag, tossed in her backpack, then closed the flap.

"Is that so bears don't get in?" asked Wesley, watching as she pulled down the zipper. His voice sounded somewhat worried.

"It's so mosquitoes don't get in." Mae answered. "Okay—done! Let's explore!"

They scrambled up and around the ledges.

"Let's stay away from there," Mae said, pointing up the slope. "There's always been a coyote den by those rocks, and I don't want to disturb them. The coyotes will have babies now, and we should leave them alone."

"Coyotes is BAD!" said Wesley, with a look of fear in his eyes.

"No, they're not," said Mae. "Why would you say that, Wesley?"

"'Cuz my dad said so. He told me. He said they kill all the deer and rabbits that we need to eat and that they would kill me too!"

"Oh, that's not really true," said Mae. "Yes, they eat rabbits, that's right. But they don't eat lots of deer—just some fawns sometimes. And they are very scared of people. If you see a coyote when you're by yourself, just stand up as tall as you can and yell at it. It will run away."

"But Dad says they're bad! He says we should shoot them all! Bang! Bang! Bang!" Wesley extended his thumb and index finger and pointed toward the rocks.

"Well, I know some people don't like coyotes. It's just because they don't know about them. Coyotes are good mommies and daddies who raise their babies with lots of love. The whole family lives together—even aunts and uncles, too. Do you have aunts or uncles?"

"Yep. Aunt Carol sends us Christmas presents!"

"Do you ever see her?"

"No, she lives someplace else. Dad says when he has enough money we can go visit, but not for a long time."

"Oh. Well, the coyote aunts and uncles live with the mommies and daddies and everybody takes care of the babies. They feed them and play with them and teach them how to hunt."

"But aren't you a-scared?" Wesley asked, his eyes wide with fear.

"Scared of what, sweetie?"

"That they'll eat you! That they'll come into your tent at night and eat you! I don't want them to eat you!" Wesley started crying.

"No, no, Wesley!" Mae pulled him close and hugged him and rocked him.

"They won't hurt me, I promise! They want to stay away from me. They're afraid of me. Oh, Wesley, my little pirate, it's okay, I'll be fine."

Wesley pulled away, sniffling; his mask was down around his chin, and his eye patch was pushed up on his forehead. His weak eye slid downward toward his nose.

"Are you sure?" he asked earnestly. "Are you sure they won't hurt you or kill you? 'Cuz if they do, I will kill them!"

he vowed. His frightened and solemn plea brought tears to Mae's eyes. She hugged him again.

"Wesley, I promise you, cross my heart, they won't pay any attention to me at all! Please believe me, okay? And I never want you to hurt them, okay?"

"Awright."

"Awright."

Some days, when Wesley didn't meet Mae at the pond, he and Jack walked down the dirt road from his house to the bridge where it met the main road to the Allen farm. If it was near lunchtime, his dad's friend Luis might be at the bridge, contemplating the cold, rushing stream while he smoked his cigarettes. Some days James walked down with Wesley and Jack; then he and Luis would talk while Wesley threw sticks into the stream. Usually Wesley didn't listen, but sometimes he overheard bits of their conversations about Mexico or the weather. More recently, they talked about COVID with worried looks on their faces.

Wesley and Jack showed up by themselves one day.

"Como esta, mi amigo?" Luis asked.

"Como. Esta. Mi Migo," Wesley slowly repeated back to him.

Luis had friendly brown eyes and a very big smile. He was Wesley's best friend in the whole world, next to Jack. Sometimes Luis shared his lunch with Wesley and tossed scraps to the dog.

Wesley saw that Luis had a pile of sticks all set to go, stacked against the upstream side of the bridge.

"You ready, mi amigo?" Luis asked.

Wesley threw a stick in the water, then raced to the other side and watched for it to emerge under the bridge and float downstream. Then he ran back to the pile and threw in another one.

Luis finished his cigarette and joined the game. They dashed back and forth to see whose stick was fastest. Jack dashed back and forth, too, until he ran down the bank and leaped into the water, ending the game by catching their sticks.

"My lunch break's over, Wesley," said Luis. "I gotta get back to the water building."

"Awready?" whined Wesley. "What do you do there, anyway?"

"I drive a machine called a forklift. It has two big forks that stick out in front. I drive it forward and slide the forks under a heavy wooden pallet that's stacked with lots of water bottles, and then I have to figure out where to put them."

"Wow!" said Wesley. "That sounds like fun!"

"Yeah, I guess sometimes it is. It's kind of like putting together a great big jigsaw puzzle. Okay maybe I'll see ya mañana, amigo. Adios!"

Luis Salavar turned and walked back to work. He thought about how crowded the warehouse was and how nice it would be to have more room. When big orders came in, there were lots of pallets to move. Then space got tight, and it was hard to maneuver through the warehouse. The solution, of course, was to add on to the building, but Luis didn't think the boss would go for it.

Charlie Glantz stepped out of his office and scanned the

warehouse. He spotted Luis coming in the door.

"Luis," he called, "I just told Juan to ramp up our output! We got the bid on 50 Rite-Buy stores! Make room on the floor—production's going up!"

Luis looked desperately across the warehouse. Where the hell was he going to put 15 percent more cases of water bottles? Even if he used the empty box trailers for some of the overage, he'd still run out of room. He was a good worker, and he knew Glantz appreciated his hard work. But he had no doubts about his expendability or that of any other workers in the plant. If Luis couldn't find room for the water, Glantz would fire him and hire someone who would.

CHAPTER FIFTEEN

Mae, July 2020

Mae followed Wesley and Jack along the old jeep trail through the woods. The day was hot; the air was thick and humid even in the shade of the trees. She was five months pregnant, and although she was starting to look a little pudgy, the bigger difference was her lack of stamina. She had to move slower, and it was harder to catch her breath. Otherwise, she felt fine. Eating and sleeping were no problem at all, and she made sure she got out for a long hike or bike ride every day.

Wesley stopped to look down at a little orange salamander on the trail.

"Oh, good find, Wesley! E is for eft!"

"E is for F?" he asked with some suspicion.

"No, eft. E-F-T. Eft. Isn't it cute?"

They picked it up and looked at its smiley little face.

"These little salamanders hatch out of tiny eggs in ponds. Then when they get older, they crawl out of the water and live on land for a few years. Then they go back into the water as adult newts and lay their eggs. First they're efts, then they're newts! E is for eft, N is for newt!"

Wesley bent down to release the eft, then watched it slowly work its way under a fern. Mae sat down on a large rock to catch her breath. He came and sat next to her. He looked distressed.

"Do you have any paper?" he asked hesitantly, looking down at the ground.

Mae looked at him questioningly.

"Paper? What for, sweetie?"

"I can't tell you."

Tears started to fill Wesley's eyes. His face was red.

"What is it, honey?"

Wesley swallowed hard. "I can't tell you."

He was clearly struggling, and Mae felt bad for him.

"Can you whisper it?" she asked.

He nodded.

Mae bent her ear next to his mouth.

"I have to go to the bathroom," she barely heard.

"Number two?" Mae whispered back. Wesley nodded.

Mae straightened up and said confidently, "Well, that's easy, my pirate friend! Come with me."

Mae walked over to a level spot behind a tree. Wesley followed.

"Look, Wesley. Dig out a little hole with the heel of your shoe in the dirt and leaves, like this. When you go, aim for that hole, and when you're done, use your foot to cover it back over with the stuff you moved out of the way. Just try not to touch any of it."

"What about paper?" Wesley asked, a little less embarrassed.

Mae plucked some large leaves from a nearby tree and handed them to Wesley.

"These will work fine. Now, I'll go back to sit on that rock, and you come join me when you're done, okay? And let me know if you need more leaves or anything."

When Wesley rejoined her, Mae said, "Okay, it's time for a little survival lesson."

As they walked along the trail, Mae picked different kinds of leaves.

"There are lots of leaves in the woods, Wesley. Some of them are good to use, some are not very comfortable. When you know you have to go, get leaves that are kind of big if you can, but always find some that are smooth and soft. This is what you just used. It's called striped maple."

They arrived back at the pond. Wesley gave Mae a big hug and ran home. Mae turned toward the farmhouse, shook her head, and smiled.

Jenny showed up one Friday afternoon with a bag of groceries and a box of maternity clothes. With the preserves from the cellar, Mae needed fewer supplies. Toilet paper was still in short supply, but Jenny managed to bring a roll or two each visit.

"Have you thought about getting the phone company to hook up the old landline? How are you going to let anyone know when you're going to have the baby?" asked Jenny.

"Well," said Mae, "I don't think I can afford a phone now, but with you swinging by once in a while, I think it will work out okay."

"All right," said Jenny. "I can't help you out right now—money's a bit tight for us too, but sometime you should probably consider it. You feeling okay?"

"Yep! I'm sleeping well and I feel great. I can still ride the bike, and I'm gardening a lot—there's always a bunch of weeding to do. I think everything's good!"

"Okay, then, let me know if you need me. Hugs!"

"Hugs to you too, Jen. Oh, here's your money." Mae handed Jenny two twenties. "Thank you so much, and say hi to Ben and the girls for me."

Mae went inside to put away the groceries. Ooh, cookies! Jenny was always slipping in little surprises. She looked in the box of clothing. Most of it was still too big, but Mae's stomach was expanding, and she welcomed the elastic-waisted pants. She wondered how much longer she'd be riding the bike, and she thought about what she needed to get done before her mobility decreased.

I'd better get up in the attic before I get any bigger, she thought. She'd been finding little treasures throughout the house, and there were bound to be things she could use up there. Getting into the attic, though, took some athletic ability.

The entrance into the attic was halfway up the stairs, at the landing. There was a half door at waist height she had to reach up to unlatch, then swing open. Then she had to swing herself up through the door and land with her butt on the bottom of the doorway, and swing her legs around to the attic floor; then she could stand up. The low ceiling meant hunching over the whole time, and she remembered that in the summer, the attic was hot and stuffy and made her feel claustrophobic.

It had always been an exciting place, filled with historic family treasures from long before Mae had been born. When they were kids, she and Gary had enjoyed playing up there, along with the added challenges of entering and exiting the little room.

Mae managed to hop up and get in. She reached toward the ceiling to turn the bare lightbulb; it still worked. She found the old globe, the one Oma had used to teach Mae world geography, and placed it by the door. The big cedar chest was still there. So was the old crystal punch bowl set. And a metal high chair that first Maggie, then Mae, had used for their dolls.

She spotted an old tie-dyed T-shirt that Cyrus had given to Buddy for Christmas one year, and she put that with the globe to take downstairs.

Hopping down out of the attic was easier than getting in, but Mae couldn't imagine that Buddy and Oma had vaulted themselves in and out of the little door until just a few years before.

When Mae reached the kitchen, she heard James's battered truck pull up to the house. She smiled, thinking of him and Wesley and Jack, and what a sweet little family they were. It broke her heart that Wesley's mom was gone, but James was doing the best he could and he seemed to be doing a pretty good job.

She stepped outside to greet them and was surprised to see Wesley and Jack sitting in the truck. James strode angrily toward her.

"What do you think you're doing, undermining me to my son?" James demanded.

Mae stepped back, stunned. "What, what are you talking about? What do you mean?" she stuttered.

"You told him that I'm a liar! You told Wesley that I was wrong about coyotes, and now he doesn't believe me! What right do you have to cut me down in front of him?" His face was red.

"James!" exclaimed Mae," I never, never said you were a liar. I never would do anything to make Wesley think less of you! Can we please sit down and talk about this?"

"No!" yelled James. "I don't think we can. I want you to stay away from Wesley. You upset him, and I don't want you near him!" With that, James jumped into the truck and slammed it into reverse. Mae watched in dismay as Wesley started crying and waved to her. James turned the truck around and floored the gas all the way down the driveway.

Production at the water plant had revved up. Shifts worked around the clock to fill the trailers of the semitrucks that sped up and down the valley road.

Space at the warehouse was tight, as Luis knew it would be. He'd been able to stagger storage in some of the unused trailer beds. He knew it wasn't a good solution, but Glantz was never going to sink more capital into expanding the building. As he stood on the bridge, finishing his lunch and gazing into the stream, Luis could not figure out how he was going to fit more bottles into the warehouse. There was just no remaining space. Maybe he could talk Glantz into purchasing some more trailers.

Suddenly Luis thought of the docks. Why hadn't he thought of them before? The two abandoned loading docks behind the warehouse were old. But by reinforcing their footings with concrete, he could make the space usable again, and he could store at least a third more cases out there. It was the only solution that made sense.

Luis hurried up the road to the warehouse. He would

go right to Glantz with his plan. With one of the other guys helping him, it would take less than a day to install heavy floor jacks to support the weight of the pallets until they could get the concrete poured.

As Luis entered the warehouse, he heard the whine of the forklift. Why was it running? He was supposed to be the only forklift operator working that day.

Between the rows of pallets, he saw the forklift moving a load of full water bottles toward the rear of the warehouse. He didn't recognize the driver.

"Hey, who are you?" Luis yelled, but his voice was lost in the noise of the forklift, along with the whirr and bang of the water bottling equipment.

He finally did it, he thought as he ran toward the forklift. *Glantz hired a replacement for me. I can't lose my job! How'm I gonna support my family?*

Luis felt desperation rising as he neared the forklift. He waved his arms to get the driver's attention, and the machine quieted.

"Who are you?" shouted Luis. "Why are you driving my forklift?"

"I'm your replacement. Sorry, buddy, but your boss needs someone who can do the work. He told me to move in more cases."

"But what are you gonna do with them? There's no place to put them!"

"Well, then, *Seen-yor amee-go,*" the driver sneered, "I guess I'll just have to get creative!" And he fired the forklift back up.

Luis was stunned. Had Glantz replaced him? Halfway

through his shift? He started toward the office. Maybe he was overreacting. Maybe he wasn't fired. He had to tell Glantz that the loading docks were the only storage space left and that he could quickly get them into shape.

That guy, Luis thought, approaching Glantz's door. *What did he mean about getting creative?* Luis turned to look back at the forklift. He saw that the driver had opened the sliding door to the outside docks.

No. No! He couldn't—the docks weren't strong enough—they wouldn't hold the weight of the forklift!

Luis ran back across the warehouse. He yelled and waved his arms, but just as before, his voice was drowned out by all the other noises. The forklift was nearing the open doorway. The driver couldn't see Luis; his view was blocked by the pallet of cases on the forks. Luis lunged for the sliding door and hauled it across the opening.

Too late, the driver saw the door close in front of him and tried to hit the brake. Instead, his foot pushed the throttle forward. The forklift accelerated into Luis and pinned him against the door.

Luis first felt the wooden pallet smash into his pelvis. Then the weight of the water bottles was propelled into his chest; more than 2,000 pounds crushed his ribcage and compressed his lungs. The shocked driver finally reversed the forklift, and Luis slumped to the floor.

Charlie Glantz's office manager, on her way back from lunch, entered the front of the warehouse as the distant forklift slammed into Luis and the sliding door. She heard the crash, pulled the emergency switch, and ran to the back of the warehouse. Within 30 seconds, all the plant workers arrived at the chaotic scene. They stood helplessly in a circle as the stunned forklift operator knelt on the floor with Luis's mangled body in his arms and tears streaming down his face.

CHAPTER SIXTEEN

Ruth, July 1943

Martha's plane was off Ruth's left wing.

They'd left the army air base in Romulus, Michigan, a few days before. Weather had grounded them in Colorado Springs, where they'd waited. And waited. And waited. A dozen other women were grounded, too, most of them headed east and stuck in the same weather. For hours, Ruth bounced the silver dollar off the concrete barracks floor.

Finally, a break in the clouds and clearance to fly. The planes and knapsacks were ready to go, and Ruth and Martha were first off the tarmac. With white clouds above them and the Rockies below, Ruth breathed a long sigh and thought about her life.

Ruth had always been a loner. An old soul, more mature than most of her schoolmates. She wasn't coy and flirty like the rest of the girls. Comfortable in her own skin. Intelligent, confident and methodical, detail-oriented. In short, she was everything a good pilot needed to be.

But those qualities together had also meant few friends, none close. Martha changed that. Nearly Ruth's mirror image, Martha was more carefree. Martha brought joy and excitement to everything they did. Ruth hadn't known that life could be so much fun. And she had found her soul mate.

The pair of planes winged across Colorado and Arizona to

the army airfield in Palm Springs, California.

"Thanks for the lift, Fred!" Ruth hopped off the running board of the old truck. She'd hitched a ride back to the base after an evening out. Martha and Bill had arranged a date for Ruth with a fellow who was nice enough, but nothing special. Ruth was tired from the long day in the desert and opted to go back to the barracks, giving Martha and Bill some time alone.

Two months earlier, Martha had noticed the tall, handsome officer standing apart from the crowd. Bill could have been the center of attention in any room, but he hugged the perimeters and tried not to be noticed. He'd seemed aloof; others thought he was snobby. But Martha had sensed something different about him, and her friendly persistence eventually uncovered the shyness and insecurity that kept him from feeling comfortable in crowds. Martha made him feel confident and brought him out of his shell. They quickly became an item.
Ruth was happy to go on double dates with whatever guy Bill brought along, but there hadn't yet been anyone exceptional enough for a long-term relationship.
She was glad for Martha, she really was, but Ruth's love was flying.

She settled into her bunk and started a letter home:

Dear Mom,
 You wouldn't believe how pretty the desert is. Martha and I got back to Palm Springs yesterday. We have a couple of days off, and

*this morning we rented a car and drove up into the foothills to a ranch. We rented a couple of horses and rode up into Tahquitz Canyon. It was just like the movies! There are cactus plants and sagebrush and rocks that you can imagine bad guys hiding behind. We rode higher and higher until we reached a lake. Well, I guess it's more like a big pond. It was really hot, so we tied the horses to some scrub bushes, and swam in our skivvies. It was **Glorious**! We checked our clothes and shoes for scorpions before we put them back on, but didn't find any.*

Tonight we went to dinner with Bill—Martha's boyfriend—and one of his friends. Then they went dancing, but I felt like coming home to catch up on sleep, so here I am. I'm sure Martha won't be in for a long time, so I'm going to bed.

Give my love to Pop and anyone else who's home!

Miss you,
Ruth

CHAPTER SEVENTEEN

Wesley, July 2020

His dad was on the phone, talking in whispers. He hated when adults did that. It always meant something bad had happened.

Wesley scuffed the toes of his sneakers along the floor and headed outside with Jack. He sat on the little wooden swing hanging from the big maple behind the house and swayed back and forth, then twisted around and around one way, then let the untwisting ropes propel him around and around the other way.

Why do grownups always try to hide everything? Why can't they just say stuff? It would just be quicker to get it over with. Like taking off a Band-Aid. Wesley hated taking off Band-Aids, but he knew that a sting for two seconds is better than a whole minute of agonizing burn, and that the dread of that long painful minute is worse than the pain itself. *Just do it and get it done. Just say it and get it over with.*

Luis was dead. Just like Wesley's mother.

His father wouldn't tell him how it happened, but Wesley knew. The COVID must have killed him, like it had killed some other workers at the water plant, which he'd overheard when his Dad and Luis were talking low one day, when they hadn't known he could hear them.

Well, Wesley would just have to make more spears. And

knives. He'd have to think of more ways to guard his house.

It was a lot of pressure. His dad didn't seem to be taking it seriously. With something like the COVID around, you had to be ready. Dad didn't get more guns, he didn't practice shooting, he didn't sharpen his knives. So protecting the family would be up to Wesley.

He didn't like not being allowed to play with Mae, either. He and Jack both missed her.

I guess I should never have told my dad about the coyotes. But she seemed right! If coyote families take good care of their babies, why should we kill them? But I think I better not ever say anything that will make my dad mad again. I really messed things up.

"Come on, Wesley; we have to get to the funeral. Here's a clean shirt. Wear your good pants. We can't do much about your sneakers, but nobody will care."

Wesley had never seen his father look like this. He'd shaved, and he was wearing a new shirt that had buttons down the front. They'd both scrubbed their hair and faces and fingernails; now James's nails were almost free of grease, and Wesley's were almost free of dirt.

They told Jack to stay home, and got into the truck, and willed it to start. It did.

Six miles down the road, they pulled into the parking lot of the Congregation of Our Lord Reformed Church. Because of the pandemic, the funeral couldn't be held inside, so James and Wesley and 37 other mourners assembled in the adjacent cemetery.

Luis's co-workers were there, and folks from the church. Some other townspeople, and Ernesto and Mariella Martina, too.

Wesley had never been to a funeral before. At least, not one he could remember. His mom's funeral didn't count because he didn't remember it. Not quite. But, maybe, somewhere back in his brain was a part that did.

Wesley looked at the people around him. Some had masks on, and he didn't know if he recognized them or not. Wesley had his mask on, and his eye patch. They made him feel close to Mae.

The service started, and Wesley burrowed a little into his dad's side. There were lots of words. Then more words. Then some singing. He could see Luis's family in front by the coffin—the two children and their mother, silently sobbing. Wesley didn't know the children, but he'd like to. The boy looked a little older than he was, and the girl looked younger.

There were more words, and singing again, and then it was over. People started milling around, talking in low voices. Wesley walked with his father over to Luis's family, who were still crying. The little girl peeked out at Wesley from behind her mother's skirt, and the boy looked at Wesley defiantly, but with a little curiosity. Like, maybe, *I don't like that you're seeing me cry. But someday maybe we could play together.* Wesley's dad gently said some things to the mom, then shook the boy's hand and patted the girl on her shoulder.

As they walked to the parking lot, his dad took Wesley's hand and held it so tight that it hurt.

When they reached the truck, Wesley saw the bicycle leaning against the fence.

"Mae's here!" he yelled, and then he remembered his dad was mad at Mae. He probably shouldn't have said that. He looked around and saw her on the side of the church lawn, talking to Mrs. Allen. Before Wesley knew what he was doing, he wriggled his fingers free and tore across the lawn.

"Mae! Mae!" he yelled, wrapping his arms around her waist when he reached her. James came along behind him.

Mae had arrived just after the service started. She'd held back from the crowd, knowing the local resistance to mask-wearing and wondering that a public funeral was even taking place. So she'd tried to be unobtrusive. She'd seen James standing in the middle of the group of mourners with Wesley's head burrowed under his arm. Mae imagined how hard it would be for James to go to a funeral again after his wife's death. He'd never confided to her about it, but it was plain from Wesley's bits and pieces that they'd been a happy, loving family.

When the service ended, Mae thought she could inconspicuously slip away. But Mrs. Allen had spied her walking away, and called her back and started asking questions that leaned suspiciously toward "Are you pregnant?" without actually coming out and asking. While Mae attempted to avoid giving conclusive answers, Wesley had run up and embraced her, and now here came James.

Mae felt disoriented. The funeral had been deeply sorrowful. She hadn't known Luis, but she'd waved to him at the bridge a few times when she'd ridden her bike to the farm. Mrs. Allen had mentioned him with admiration—a nice man, a good worker, a gentle soul, devoted to his wife and kids. Mae knew that around here, community was everything. Everyone sticks together, everybody helps everybody else, everyone is part of a big family. So you go to parties and weddings when you're asked and to funerals to pay your respects. It wasn't until Mae had biked halfway out of the valley that she realized it would be almost impossible to avoid seeing James and Wesley. It would be very awkward, and the only way to dodge them would be to arrive late and get out of there fast.

Well, here they were; there was nothing she could do. Mae was still distressed at James's reaction toward her. Her feelings were hurt and she felt somehow responsible for his anger. And she really missed Wesley's—and James's—friendship. She hoped that James would not replay the scene at the farmhouse.

Wesley's arms wrapped tightly around her. He gazed up at her with obvious adoration, while James looked at her with a pained expression.

Oh, please don't yell at me now. Not here. It would be embarrassing and it would hurt Wesley and I might cry, so please don't, please don't.

James said quietly, "Can we talk?"

Mae was surprised. Her mood lifted. She took Wesley's hand and walked with them to the truck.

"Um, so I've been thinking," James said. "And the funeral just made things clearer. I think I was a jerk. I shouldn't have yelled at you, and I want to apologize for that. But more than that, I want to not be mad at you, and I hope I haven't lost you as a friend."

He looked so miserable that Mae's heart softened.

"Oh, James," she said, "you haven't lost me as anything! There's stuff we can talk about, but yes, the funeral was sad, and it must be so hard for you right now, and please don't feel so bad. I've missed Wesley and you both so much!"

The relief on James's face was immediate, and he broke into a smile.

"How 'bout I put your bike into the back of the truck and give you a ride home? But only if you'll go have an ice cream cone with Wes and me? I mean, you know, the Big Cone's closed, but we can probably get something at the Kari-Out."

CHAPTER EIGHTEEN

Mae, August 2020

Mae's long hours of digging, planting, and weeding finally paid off. In addition to the lettuce and peas she'd harvested early on, the garden now yielded more leafy greens and carrots, beets, and squash.

Mae loved this time of year—the few weeks left of summer before the chill of fall set in. Raspberries that had been prolific along the edge of the fields now gave way to big, sweet blackberries. Bear paths were evident through the bushes, but plenty of berries remained. The blackberries reminded Mae of Gram's pies. She could almost hear the sizzle of the bluish-black gooey sweetness bubbling through the over-full crust and dripping onto the oven floor. Almost see and smell, almost touch and taste Gram's pie in front of her. She and Gramps could eat a whole pie between them.

Mae worried about her dwindling roll of cash. She was grateful that the land was giving her most of what she needed to eat. She could preserve a lot of the vegetables from the garden, along with berries and applesauce if she bought some canning jars and supplies. She could also check for empty jars in the cellar.

Nights would soon be cold again, and she'd need to buy a few loads of firewood for the winter. Mae was grateful that Oma and Buddy were paying the electric bill, and she knew there must be taxes and insurance payments, too. Oma had assured her that they were just happy the house was being lived in, happy that Mae was there. Still, she felt guilty about not contributing.

And what about after the baby came? There would definitely be expenses. Mae didn't really know what babies need. She knew she couldn't afford disposable diapers, though Jenny had offered to give her the cloth diapers her daughters had used. There were still diaper covers to buy, but that was a one-time purchase. She would breastfeed the baby, so no expense there.

Mae was also concerned about how to care for an infant. The idea of a baby was foreign to her. She'd never been around small children, and she really couldn't imagine what it would be like to have a tiny, helpless being that she was responsible for and had to take care of. *How will I know when to change the diaper? How do I give it a bath? How often should I breastfeed? What if it cries all the time?* She asked Jenny a lot of questions, and she knew Jenny was often amused by them.

Must be kind of like having a puppy, she thought, although she'd never had one of those, either.

What else? Mae finally faced the real question that she had been avoiding for months: having the baby. The actual birth. Mae had put off thinking about it, just because it had seemed so far in the future. But now that she was feeling bulky, Mae knew she really should make a plan.

She didn't want to go to a hospital. According to the radio, COVID cases were rampant in the cities, and she had no reason to think they weren't out here in the country, as well.

She didn't want to go to a doctor's office, and as long as she felt well and took her prenatal vitamins, she didn't think she needed to. So how was she going to do this?

Everyone knew that the Allen kids had been born at home, and Jenny said that Mrs. Allen had assisted a local midwife for a few years.

I guess I'll go see Mrs. Allen, thought Mae. *From the comments she made to me at Luis's funeral, she obviously already suspects that I'm pregnant.*

Mae rode the bike up to the Allen farm. She needed eggs anyway and thought she could somehow work the subject of her pregnancy into a casual conversation. For some reason, she felt embarrassed admitting it to Mrs. Allen—to anyone, really. Was she embarrassed because she was pregnant? Or because she let herself get pregnant? She didn't know how the people who had known her from her childhood would judge her. They were of a different generation, and in many ways, Mae felt like she was 12 years old again when she was around them.

She stopped at the milk house first. She put a ten in the box, took two dollars in change, and put two dozen eggs in the basket on the back of her bike. She pushed the bike up to the farmhouse, put on her mask, and knocked.

Mrs. Allen came to the door, wiping flour from her hands onto her apron.

"Hi, Mae. Come on in. Casper's finishing his lunch, and I just put two pies in the oven."

Mae followed Mrs. Allen into the kitchen. Just like Gram's used to be. Mixing bowls filled the sink, and flour dusted the countertop. Mr. Allen had raised the last of a sandwich to his mouth.

"Oh, hi, Mae," he said. He shoved it in and swallowed.

"I'm on my way out to cut the hayfield over by your place. That bike still working okay?"

"Oh, yes, thank you. It's great."

He pushed his chair back from the table and put his plate in the sink. He bent down and gave his wife a peck on the cheek.

"Can't wait to have a piece of pie later, Patsy. I'll be thinking about it all afternoon."

Mrs. Allen said, "It'll be waiting for you, Casper." She wiped up the flour from the counter.

"Oh, sorry, Mae, let me put on my mask. Now, what can I do for you?"

"I don't know how to ask you this, Mrs. Allen. I . . . um . . . ah . . ."

"Honey, what is it? Come sit down." Mrs. Allen guided Mae to a chair at the table and sat across from her. "What's the matter?"

"Well, nothing is really the *matter*, really, it's just that I'm um . . . well, I'm *pregnant*," said Mae.

"Hmm. Well, I thought so," said Mrs. Allen.

"I thought maybe you had guessed, from our conversation at Luis's funeral."

"Yep. You've been looking a little . . . *heftier* lately. And not quite as . . . *sprightly* as a few months ago. I know the look. How far along are you?"

"Should be six months now. It was um . . . Valentine's Day. Night."

"Okay. So what's your plan?"

"Well, I don't really want to go to a doctor. I feel fine, and Jenny got me some prenatal vitamins. I'm eating well, and I think I'm doing okay. And I *really* don't want to go to a hospital to have the baby. I'd hate to go in and catch COVID. And have the baby get it, too."

"Oh, boy," said Mrs. Allen. "I think I know what you're going to ask me."

"Mrs. Allen, would you help me? Will you deliver the baby? I really don't know what else to do." Tears welled up in Mae's eyes. She felt alone, she felt very uncomfortable, and she thought Mrs. Allen was going to say no.

Patsy Allen's heart went out to Mae. This girl, this young woman who looked like a girl, was all alone and in need. Throughout the spring and summer she had worked hard at that old farmhouse to straighten it up, to make it a home, to plant a garden. She never asked for help, and not only had she survived, she had thrived. This little girl had grown into a young woman who was strong like her grandmother and great-grandmother, and now she needed another strong woman to help her through this. How could she say no?

"Of course, Mae, I'll help you. Together we'll deliver this baby. Here's what we need to do."

Mrs. Allen gave Mae a rundown of what to expect and what they would need. As they talked, a weight lifted from Mae's shoulders. She was elated. She had help. She had a plan. She knew what she needed to do to get ready for the baby. For the first time since she'd moved into the farmhouse, Mae no longer felt alone. She rose from the table to leave.

"Just one more thing, Mae," said Mrs. Allen. "Have you told

your family?"

Mae sat back down.

"No," she said. "I haven't dared."

"Well, there's the phone. I'll be outside."

A feeling of dread came over Mae as she punched in the number. She was nervous and couldn't even think of how she would start the conversation.

Well, Oma has a way of making things easier, she thought. *I'll say it fast and see what happens.*

The phone rang five times.

Once more and I'll hang up, she thought, with a feeling of relief. Then someone picked up.

"Hello?"

Mae didn't say anything.

"Hello?"

She didn't want to say anything. Instead of Oma, Maggie had answered. Why had Maggie answered? She never answered the phone. Mae hadn't even considered the possibility, and now Maggie was on the line. Should she hang up? Just hang up and try again tomorrow?

"Hello? Who is this?" asked Maggie, sounding irritated.

"It's me. Maggie, it's me. Mae."

"Well, hi, sweetheart!" gushed Maggie. "I haven't heard from you in a long time! How are you, pumpkin?"

"I'm doing pretty good, Maggie." Mae tried to gauge Maggie's sobriety. She didn't sound slurry or sloppy. Maybe she was clean. Mae didn't want to give her the benefit of the doubt, though, just in case.

"How's Oma? And Buddy?"

"They're really good, honey! They've been driving me to my meetings and keeping the place clean and cooking for me and Cyrus. It's really nice to have them here."

Mae realized how much she missed her family. And even talking to Maggie wasn't so bad. But she didn't want to tell Maggie her news.

"Where's Oma?"

"She went to the store. She said she'll be back in a little while. Cy's at work and Buddy's fishin'."

Mae thought maybe she could chat a bit, just until Oma came back. Maybe she could talk to Maggie; they hadn't spoken in a long time. Hearing Maggie again softened Mae, made her wish they could reconnect. Now that she was going to have a baby, she realized how important a mother's advice could be. Maybe she could ask Maggie what it was like to have a baby. Maybe she could take a chance.

"Um, Maggie? Did you like being pregnant?"

"Hell, no!" Maggie howled. "I was sick all the time and bigger than a cow! I had to give up partyin' till after the baby was born, and then it woke up and cried all night and wouldn't let me get any sleep. It was terrible. Worst time of my life!"

Tears welled into Mae's eyes.

Oh, no, you don't, Mae thought. *Damn it, Maggie. Do you even know who you're talking to? Don't you know that you're saying things a mother should never say to her child?*

Mae steeled her heart, as she used to do, all the time. She steeled her voice.

"Never mind, Maggie," she said. "You go back to sleep or whatever you've been doing and just tell Oma I called."

Mae hung up fast and hard.

"I left a message," she choked out to Mrs. Allen as she rushed to her bike.

She was hurt and angry all the way back to the farmhouse. The black mood stayed with her the next day, and the next. She hadn't felt this way since last time. She knew she should have hung up when she'd first heard Maggie's stupid voice.

CHAPTER NINETEEN

Ruth, August 1943

Ruth and Martha were up in the sky, Martha off Ruth's left wing.

The P-63 Kingcobra was a stable, well-built aircraft—in essence, a heavier, modified version of the P-51. The increased weight was not a worrisome flying consideration; in fact, after leveling off, the P-63 handled more responsively than several of the other planes they'd been flying. Its fortified fuselage enabled it to be used in low-level fighting, but the increased weight also limited its agility and forgiveness in evasive maneuvering, especially in aerial dives.

They'd picked up the P-63s in Niagara Falls and were headed for Great Falls, Montana.

It was good to be up in the air again. The long trip to Niagara Falls had started in Nebraska, where Ruth and Martha picked up B-29s for delivery to MacDill army airfield in Florida. The delivery had been a piece of cake, but then the snafu began.

"I swear, Ruthie, Fifinella's hiding in my pocket. Couldn't we have gotten lucky and caught a hop heading north outta here?"

They'd almost had a ride on a flight from MacDill to the Great Lakes. The pilot's orders had changed at the last minute and left them stranded in Florida, and it would be three days, at least, before another flight went north. So they decided to take the train, but they could only afford two seats to Baltimore. After some frantic phone calls with Martha's Aunt Eunice, it was arranged that Martha's cousin in Baltimore would meet them at the station. She would bring sandwiches and buy their tickets through to Niagara Falls.

That night, when they disembarked at Baltimore, Cousin Katherine was nowhere to been seen, even after two hours of waiting.

"Martha, do you think we should have headed through Atlanta instead of Baltimore? Maybe we could have gotten to Buffalo sooner."

"I thought of that, Ruthie, but the next train to Atlanta wasn't till tonight, and I thought this would be faster."

Ruth was hungry and tired.

"Well, I guess it wasn't faster, was it? I think we screwed up."

"Aw, Ruthie, it'll be all right. Sit back and relax."

Martha went to the payphone.

"Hello, Aunt Eunice, oh, yes, operator." Silence, while the operator asked Aunt Eunice if she would accept the charges. "Yes, thank you, operator. Hello, Aunt Eunice, this is Martha again. I'm sorry I had to reverse the charges. Yes, thank you. Aunt Eunice, we've been here at the station for two hours and Katherine hasn't shown up. No. Okay, I'll wait." Martha looked at Ruth, then up at the ceiling while she waited for her aunt to look for the notes she'd scribbled the day before.

"Yes, Aunt Eunice, no, it's okay, but do you know where she is? What? No, no! I said today! I said we'd be getting in tonight, not tomorrow night! She what? She did? Oh, no! Is there any way to reach her? Well, we don't know anyone here, and we're kind of stuck." Silence. Martha shot Ruth a worried look.

"Okay, Aunt Eunice, thank you. No, that's okay. I'll let you know if we do. Okay, I appreciate your help. Good-bye."

Martha looked at Ruth again.

"Aunt Eunice says that Katherine thought we were leaving Florida tomorrow, so she's planning to meet us tomorrow night."

"Well, can't we call Katherine and have her come get us now?" Ruth asked.

"Nope. She had to go to New York for work today and she's staying over. So it looks like we're on our own."

It was late and the station was empty. No more trains headed north for the night.

"Grab a bench, Ruthie. It's just an adventure. Let's get some sleep; I have a plan."

They each stretched out on a bench, put their jackets over their heads, and tried to sleep.

The next morning, Ruth uncovered her head at the sound of the bustle of the station. Martha had disappeared. When she finally showed up, she seemed fresh as a daisy and was smiling broadly.

"It's about time you woke up! Hey, guess what? The stationmaster, who has a son in the army, has heard of us women pilots. Ruthie, he personally paid our fare all the way through! We'll be on the next train to New York, then switch trains to Albany, where we have a final switch to Niagara

Falls. It'll be a long trip, but we'll get there. And he bought us boxed lunches too!"

Twenty-four hours later, Winston Churchill and his daughter Mary also disembarked at the Niagara Falls train station. While the two Churchills viewed the falls and enjoyed a special luncheon held in their honor, Ruth and Martha were on their way to pick up their planes at the Bell factory. Had the three women crossed paths, they'd have found common ground in the service of their countries' war efforts. Mary Churchill also wore a uniform, the British Army uniform of the antiaircraft battery she commanded in England.

Finally in the air, Martha and Ruth hugged their planes along the Lake Erie shoreline to Cleveland, then tacked toward Chicago, and finally headed northwest for North Dakota.

Ruth kept a weather eye to the sky. The day was bright; no threat of rain, a few high puffs, but no storm clouds on the horizon. She glanced to her left at Martha's plane. She wished they could fly on forever.

At 12,000 feet over Minneapolis, Ruth's first fuel tank was running low and she flipped the toggle to switch over to the second tank. Within seconds, the engine sputtered, then died. With no lift, no air rushing beneath its wings to keep the plane aloft, the nose began to dip and the aircraft began to fall.

Training scenarios raced through Ruth's mind. She needed to figure out why the engine had stalled and at the same time restart the plane. Calm as ever, she tackled both problems simultaneously.

The engine stalled when I switched tanks. I need to spin the prop.

Ruth reached over and flipped the toggle back to the first tank. Concurrently, she pushed the nose down into a dive. Although she'd practiced the maneuver multiple times, Ruth knew that her chances of survival were dropping proportionally with her altitude.

The P-63 shuddered as it dove vertically toward the ground. With one eye on the altimeter, Ruth prayed that the plane would pick up enough speed to windmill the propeller and restart the engine. Maintaining control of the plane was made difficult by its bulk. Ruth didn't know it at the time, but the P-63's weight distribution made it susceptible to entering into a flat spin, from which recovery was almost impossible.

Her hands gripped the control column so hard that they hurt. She watched the needle spin: 10,000 feet. 8,000. 5,000. Ruth's mouth was dry. The ground—the roads, the fields, the green of it—suddenly seemed closer, much closer. She would dive straight into it; she would die if she could not restart the engine.

Finally, finally, the propeller whirled. The engine sputtered and finally caught, and Ruth gently eased the column back. She leveled the plane at 2,000 feet.

She climbed up to 5,000. She thought she would be sick. It passed. She squared her shoulders and breathed deeply. Martha swung in on the left and they continued on a northwest heading until they could safely touch down at the Hector Airfield in Fargo, North Dakota.

"Ruthie!" Martha had hurried over to Ruth's plane. "Come on, let's get you out of there."

Ruth climbed out of the cockpit, her legs unsteady on the

ground. The palm of her left hand was wrapped around the silver dollar in her pocket. Her fingertips felt the outline of the girl's face.

Ruth gave Martha a weak grin.

"I hope I never have to do that again."

"Ruthie, if any of us could pull that off, it's you," said Martha. "I guess Fifinella ended up in *your* pocket. Damn, you did a great job! Let's go get a cup of coffee."

The airfield mechanics took the second fuel tank apart and inspected it, along with the fuel lines. They discovered that the Bell factory ground crew had neglected to remove the plug from the second tank's fuel line. The fuel simply was not able to flow to the engine.

Problem solved, Ruth and Martha climbed back into their cockpits and took off again. Four hours later they touched down in Montana. The American women were not allowed to fly across the US border. From Great Falls the planes would be ferried across Canada by American male pilots, then handed off in Alaska to female Russian pilots who ferried them on to Siberia to be used by the Russians against the German invasion.

"You know, Ruthie," said Martha, "it would make a whole lot more sense if they'd just let us fly to Alaska."

"I know, Marth. But we're in the army. Sense doesn't count."

CHAPTER TWENTY

Wesley, August 2020

Wesley and Jack raced to the pond. They chased frogs into the water and splashed after them. After a while they climbed out and lay in the sun. Wesley noticed that some of the leaves in the trees around the pond were turning red. He hadn't lived enough summers to recognize the turning point—the day in late summer that flirts with fall, when shorts are about to give way to jeans, when swimming is almost over for this year and won't be back for five or six months into the next.

Wesley just knew that he and Jack were happy. They'd had fun and gotten soaked, and as long as he didn't think too much about it, life was good.

Suddenly the *whoosh whoosh whoosh* started up across the valley. The COVID must have woken up, and Wesley was afraid. He fumbled in his pocket for his mask and slipped the loops over his ears. Mae had said he needed it to keep the COVID away when he was around other people. That didn't make any sense at all; he was the most scared when he was alone. So Wesley carried the mask with him all the time. He figured he should wear it whenever he knew the COVID was nearby.

Thoughts whirled through his brain. Everything sad and scary converged on him at once. The CANCER had made his mother sick. That his mother died from it translated into *the CANCER got her*. Now the COVID was gasping, probably coming to get him and Jack and his dad.

He thought of the cache of spears hidden in the bushes behind the barn and felt a little better. He thought of the sharp stick knives rolled into a shirt in the back of his closet. He'd spent a long time cutting and sharpening each one and was very proud of them. Every night after his dad tucked him in, Wesley silently slipped from between the sheets and carefully arranged his knives in a circle around the bed, tips pointed outward. He then put the sharpest one under his pillow and climbed back into bed. Only this nightly ritual, and Jack curled up on the bed, allowed Wesley to fall asleep. Every morning he quietly put his weapons away before going downstairs.

Wesley looked over at Jack, stretched out on the warm ground next to him. As long as Jack wasn't alarmed, Wesley felt better. The COVID wasn't close enough to hurt him. Not yet.

CHAPTER TWENTY-ONE
Mae, September 2020

The washing machine was dead. Mae had loaded her dirty clothes, poured in the detergent, pushed the start button, and nothing happened. She turned the knob, tried again, nothing. A third time, nothing.

Damn, she thought.

She'd known the machine was on its way out when Gram was still living there. Mae was lucky it had worked at all during the past seven months.

Aw, crap. It'll cost a few hundred dollars to replace. Okay, I can wash everything in the sink. My stuff's easy. But what about after the baby comes? What then, Fifi?

Mae didn't have a lot of options. She couldn't ask Oma and Buddy for more money; they were already taking care of the house bills and the taxes. And the insurance.

She didn't want to ask Mr. Allen or James for help. What could they do, anyway? Buddy had limped the machine along for Gram for years. He'd already replaced everything on it he could, at least once. The problem would just have to resolve itself.

She scrubbed her clothes in the sink and hung them on the line.

Then, out to the garden to see what she should can first. Jenny had dropped off pickling spices and two boxes of new jars, and Mae's money was just about gone.

The carrots were getting big and kind of tough. She could chop up dozens of them and can several jars for herself, and then mash some up for baby food. She wanted to get the squashes done before they got too big; she could can some and pickle a bunch, too. There would still be enough left to eat through the fall.

She'd have to pickle the cucumbers soon; they were getting bigger than she wanted and wouldn't last much longer.

The green beans would be old soon, too—maybe she should start with those.

And the blackberries! She'd need to get after what was left and preserve what she could for her winter dessert.

For the next several days, Mae picked, pickled, cooked, and canned. When she wasn't in the garden gathering vegetables, she was in the fields trying to coax the last of the blackberries out from hiding. She picked newly ripened apples to make quarts and quarts of applesauce. Evenings were spent cooking whatever she'd harvested that day, then spooning the results into jars and finishing them in the water bath.

Mae honestly didn't know how she knew what she was doing. She'd spent lots of time in the kitchen while Oma and Gram were canning, but she didn't remember helping. Most of the time she'd simply hung out with them, talking and watching as the food was cooked and the jars were filled.

Somehow, Mae did what she needed to, and by the time she was finished, the kitchen was overflowing with dozens of quart jars filled with every kind of food she could pick from a stem or dig from the ground. When she was finally finished, Mae started to move the jars to the cellar. She placed ten at a time into a cardboard box and carried them down the narrow stairs, and by her fourth trip, she was running out of room on the cellar shelves and out of energy as well. Mae began to shift jars around. She needed to bring up more of Gram's preserves to make space, so she took the last four jars of Gram's bread and butter pickles and placed them into the box. There was another pint of blueberry jam in the back, and then she saw a green quart jar in the corner she hadn't noticed before.

Mae pulled the jar out. It was far lighter than the others. Mae put it, along with the jar of jam, into the box and headed upstairs. She made three more trips to the cellar to store her preserves, then unpacked Gram's bounty. She put the pickles and the jam into the kitchen cabinet, then reached for the mystery jar. It weighed next to nothing, and Mae couldn't imagine what was inside.

She twisted the jar's collar and the lid slipped off. She looked inside. Her eyes widened in disbelief. She tipped the jar and pulled out the contents. Twenty- and fifty- and hundred-dollar bills spilled out over the table. She just sat still for a minute and looked at the money. Then her mind started racing.

Gram, she thought. *Gram. Holy shit. She must have socked this away for years. Lots of years. Maybe since she got married. But how? And why? And what should I do with it? Can I use it? Should I give it to Oma and Buddy? I have to tell them. This is probably their money now. But maybe I can get a new washing machine. Holy cow!*

Mae started arranging the bills. She made stacks of denominations and kept piling the bills on top of each other. Then she started counting. When she was done, she'd counted nearly $5,000 and was pretty sure she hadn't counted correctly. She was pretty sure there could be more than that.

Mae found a pen.

> Dear Oma,
> I've been canning a lot lately. It reminds me of when I was a girl, watching you and Gram putting up pickles and jams and such. I don't think I ever helped you, but I guess I learned what to do. It even smells the same!
> After I finished all the canning, I took my jars downstairs to the cellar. I had to move the rest of Gram's jars to fit mine onto the shelves. I found an old green quart jar and brought it upstairs.
> Oma, imagine my surprise when I opened it. Do you know what I found? Oma, I found about $5,000! In twenties, fifties, and hundred-dollar bills!
> I think Gram must have hidden it. Do you know anything about it?
> It's your money now, since I guess this is your house now. And you are paying for the electric bill and taxes. And insurance.
> Do you think I could use some of it to buy a washing machine, since Gram's just quit?
> Please give my love to Buddy. And Cyrus.
> I miss you so much Oma!
> Love,
> Mae

Mae wrote the address on an envelope and stuck on a stamp. She rolled up the bills and replaced them in the jar, then put the jar in the back corner of a kitchen cabinet.

She went to sleep that night and dreamed of Gram as a young woman, driving a tractor that pulled a hay wagon full of hundred-dollar bills.

Ten days later, Mae rode her bike to the Allens' farm for more eggs. She felt wild abandon as she slipped eight dollars into the container. It was the first time since she'd arrived that she wasn't almost devastatingly worried about the state of her finances. Even if Oma and Buddy needed her to wire the money to Florida, she knew they would let her have some to live on. For the first time, a burden had lifted.

Mrs. Allen put on her mask and asked Mae to lie down for a prenatal check. She listened to the baby's heartbeat, asked a few questions about Mae's diet and health, and said everything was fine.

Mae rode home, wary of the big trucks going to and from the water plant. The drivers were going faster than when she'd first arrived. Almost every time she rode to the Allens' farm she was nearly blown off the road as they blasted by.

She arrived at the mailbox as Lanore pulled up.

"Mae! It's so nice to see you!" said Lanore. "I have a letter for you, and I wanted to tell you that I saw Patsy Allen last week. She told me she'll be your midwife when you have the baby—congratulations, by the way!"

"Thanks, Lanore! I guess folks will be finding out about it. I must look like a whale on my bicycle . . . "

"No, honey, you look great! Anyway, Patsy said she wants me to keep an eye on you, since you don't have a phone or a car or anything, so if you don't mind I'll just drive down your driveway everyday as you get closer, okay? That way I can run in to check on you if I don't see you, okay? She said I should begin when you're a couple of weeks out, so when should I start?"

"Oh, gee, okay. Um, that would be . . . about the beginning of November. That was really nice of her to think of that, and so nice of you to go out of your way."

"Oh, it's exciting! I'm happy to do it, Mae, and anytime you need anything, *anything at all*, you just leave a note in the mailbox, okay? Oh, here's your letter. I gotta run, but I'll see you soon!"

Mae walked her bike up the driveway and thought about how nice everyone was to her. Her friends stuck in stuffy little apartments in New York City were probably afraid to go outside and had no opportunities to hike, or ride a bike, or garden, or make bread and butter pickles. Or get eggs from a farm. Mae felt incredibly lucky to have ended up back in the mountains.

When she got into the house, she looked at the envelope. It was from Oma. She ripped it open.

Dear, Dear Mae,

First of all, we miss you too! We often think of you alone in that old drafty farmhouse and hope you are comfortable and happy. Or at least content and safe. We are glad you don't have to see a lot of people. Down here in Florida, people are crazy. Most of our neighbors don't wear masks, they don't social distance, and they think Covid is no big deal. They are not concerned that they can get sick and die. We feel so bad for the nurses and doctors—it's not fair to them. One guy on our block just died from it, and now his family all wear masks. They didn't before. What a tragedy. It's so sad.

No, Mae—we didn't know anything about the money! Both of us are very surprised, and we agree that it must have been Gram's stash. We are perplexed—no idea where it came from or why she hid it.

We do not need the money! You can either consider it yours, since you found it, or if you would rather, you can say it belongs to the house, since that's where you found it.

In any case, use it for what you need. We know that it is costing you money to eat and buy your necessities. We also know you are careful and thoughtful so we are not worried that you will spend it foolishly. Please buy a washing machine! I'm surprised that old thing lasted this long!

Okay, honey, I love you, and Buddy wrote you a note so I'll put it in with this, too.
Everyone here says hello——even Maggie. And Cyrus sends his love.
Take care, Mae, and write again soon.
Love,
Oma

A smaller, folded note was tucked inside the letter:

Dear Mae,

You will get an important letter you might need to sign for at the post office.

After you receive it, check Gram's big cedar chest in the attic.

Now that you are a woman of means, you should buy yourself an ice cream cone once in a while. Haha!

I miss you, Maefly!
Love, Buddy

CHAPTER TWENTY-TWO

Ruth, September 1943

Ruth shifted her weight and stretched her legs as much as the tight cockpit would allow. Her neck and back were feeling strained from three hours of sitting still.

Just another hour to Pueblo, she thought, as she approached the front range of the Colorado Rockies. *Hopefully just a few minutes to fuel up and get a bite to eat, and then on my way again.*

Ruth had taken off that morning from the Palm Springs tarmac in her favorite aircraft, the fast and sexy P-51 Mustang. Some of the other planes were bulky and clumsy and awkward to handle. On one trip she'd spent four days wrestling a B-25 bomber across Texas—the longest four days of her life. But the controls, all the mechanics of the Mustang were perfectly engineered, exquisitely precise. Of everything Ruth had ever done, piloting the Mustang was the best, the very best experience she'd ever had. Her soul soared with the plane above Colorado. She felt like she could stay up here forever.

Except she couldn't. She had to deliver the Mustang to Fort Dix in New Jersey, then make her way to the Bell factory in Niagara Falls. A P-39 was waiting for transport to Montana. If she was lucky, she'd get a quick ride back to Palm Springs, or Long Beach, and then start all over again.

Morning rains had ended by the time Ruth neared Pueblo, and the sky was clear and blue. Above the Mustang, fluffy white clouds hung in the air. The airfield was minutes away.

Ruth scanned the horizon. Something out the cockpit window caught her eye. She skewed left over a wide valley in the first of the foothills that eventually led to the 12,000-foot range in the distance. She turned the plane away from the sun toward a refracted arc of colors above the valley. The top of the rainbow arched up into the sky. The colors shimmered in the sunlight. As she got closer, the rainbow grew bigger, and soon she saw the arc completed into a perfect circle beneath her. In a moment, the plane was passing though the vast, multi-hued sphere that reached toward the ground. Ruth gazed in awe at the colors that were on both sides, above, and below the little plane. Before she knew it, she was through, and the colors disappeared behind her. Ruth banked and turned back toward the sun, wanting to feel the experience again, but the angle was wrong; the rainbow was gone. Although her brain knew the science of the rainbow, there was still a mystery and magic of experiencing it so intimately for the first time, perhaps the only time in her life.

Ruth set her course for Pueblo, still amazed at how the little horsefly of a plane had flown though—*flown through!*—one of the most overwhelming displays of nature she'd ever seen. And then she remembered the clouds of her solo flight. *Grandeur!*

CHAPTER TWENTY-THREE
Wesley and Mae, September 2020

Wesley didn't go back to school the Wednesday after Labor Day. None of the students went back. They all used their computers for remote learning at home.

The school had contacted James several times about free computer time at the library in Fremont. James could barely afford gas money to run his wood operation, let alone take Wesley back and forth to the library. He knew Wesley needed the academic help, but he also knew the school year was a freakin' lost cause till COVID was under control, and Wesley wouldn't be the only one who'd have to catch up. Besides, James was playing the odds. The fewer people he and Wesley came into contact with, the less chance they'd have of getting sick.

So Wesley continued to spend his days playing with Jack and walking to the fork in the trail to meet Mae. Actually, Wesley's education wasn't lacking. He absorbed more during one day with Mae that he ever had in a week of school.

They'd already made one trip through the ABCs and were at "G is for grasshopper" in the second round. Wesley understood numbers better, too. Addition and subtraction were fun with acorns and stones.

When James had to deliver firewood farther than Fremont, Wesley and Jack stayed with Mae, and they were Wesley's favorite days. Even though Mae was getting heavier and slower, she still climbed the mountain trails. She was also teaching Wesley how to ride a small bike that Mr. Allen had found in his back shed. They went up and down the driveway, time after time. Mae slowly trotted or walked beside him, holding onto the bike, keeping him balanced, while Wesley tried to pedal and steer at the same time. Afterward, he and Jack rummaged through the barn, looking for old treasures and little critters.

Rainy days were a little harder. It was still fun to be with Mae, but sometimes Wesley got bored. One wet day at the end of September, Wesley was antsy.

"What can I do, Mae?" he whined. The rain was coming down heavy, and it looked like they'd be stuck inside all day. Jack was curled up against the sofa.

"Well, here, Wesley. Look at this book." Mae pulled out one of the old red World Book encyclopedias and showed him the spine.

"What's this letter, Wesley?"

"D!" yelled Wesley.

"Right!" yelled Mae, and she turned the pages until she found the section she was looking for.

"This was my favorite, favorite book when I was growing up," said Mae.

"Dogs!" yelled Wesley, excitedly. "I LOVE dogs!"

"I know you do, sweetie," said Mae.

Small, accurate illustrations of all sorts of dogs filled the pages. Working dogs, hunting dogs, show dogs, large dogs, toy dogs. Wesley spent nearly an hour studying the pictures, asking Mae to name each one until he had memorized almost every breed.

"Now what can we do?" he asked, when he tired of the book.

"Here, look at this," said Mae, and she placed the globe from the attic on the kitchen table. Wesley immediately started spinning it as fast as he could.

"Oh, slow down!" said Mae. "Let's not break it."

"What is it?" asked Wesley.

"It's called a globe. That means round with a map on it. See, this is the earth, you know, our planet, right? Our world. And this is how it spins around, every day, slow, like this. That's called rotation. The earth rotates. It goes around and around. This blue part is the ocean—do you know what the ocean is?"

"I heard of it before. My aunt said she had a vacation at the ocean and went swimming."

"Yep, Wesley, right! Well, the ocean is really, really big, see? All the blue part is the ocean, and all these colored places are the land, and the different colors are different countries."

Wesley's interest had waned; he just wanted to spin it around. Mae got up from the table to fix a snack.

By the time they'd finished their apples and peanut butter, the rain had stopped. The day was still gray, but they could go outside.

"Can I ride the bike?" asked Wesley.

"Sure," said Mae. "I have to check the mailbox anyway." Mae got the bike out of the barn and held it still while Wesley climbed on.

"Okay, remember to steer. Watch where you're going. And pedal. Pedal. Harder!"

They made their way up the driveway. Jack ran ahead, then back to them, then up ahead, then back again. Wesley was beginning to balance better and steer straighter.

Lanore pulled up just as they got to the mailbox.

Wesley practiced balancing on his bike while Mae held it straight and spoke to Lanore. He tried to steady himself by adjusting his body from side to side. He heard the lady tell Mae about a letter that needed to get signed; then she said she brought it so Mae didn't have to go to the post office, and gave her a pen and Mae wrote something.

Then they went back down the driveway to the house. Mae was trying to look at the envelope and didn't pay attention while she held the bike, and it almost fell over. She put the envelope into her pocket and held the bike more firmly.

Back at the house, Mae told Wesley he could play outside until lunchtime. He and Jack headed to the barn for whatever adventures they could find while Mae got a cup of tea and sat down at the kitchen table. She took the envelope out of her pocket. It was from Lewis & Lewis, Attorneys at Law. *Oh my God*, she thought. *This is probably bad news.* Then she remembered that Buddy had told her it would be arriving, and he hadn't seem alarmed, so it might not be bad news after all. Intrigued, she opened the envelope.

Dear Ms. McCain,
    This letter is to inform you that you are the

recipient of items bequeathed to you by the estate of Mr. and Mrs. Ward G. Griffin.

As of September 18th, 2020, the acreage and buildings, in their entirety, found at 85 Griffin Lane, Welby, New York, shall be entered into the tax records of the County Clerk, located at 197 Main Street, Catskill, New York, as belonging to

Miss Mae Marie McCain
85 Griffin Lane
Welby, New York

Mae was unable to read the rest of the letter. She dropped it on the table and gazed out the window. *Holy crap. Holy cow! Gram must have left the farm to me!*

In her wildest dreams, she wouldn't have thought she'd own the farm. She'd been certain that it would be left to Oma and that, of course, Oma would have to sell it.
Mae looked at the table. It was hers. The cup in front of her. The dishes in the dish rack. The chair she was sitting on. The little white eggcup.

Then she looked outside. All the land she could see was hers. What did that even mean? It meant she'd pay the land taxes. Oh, yeah, school taxes too. And the insurance. She'd be responsible for the upkeep. But she'd also be responsible for the land. For taking care of it. For making sure it was treated well. Mae welcomed the responsibility, but knew she would always feel its weight.

In a daze, she mixed up some egg salad and made sandwiches. She grabbed a jar of pickles and headed outside and called Wesley and Jack for a little picnic while the weather held.

That night when she slept it was fall and the leaves were red and orange and Mae was 14 and was carrying the .410 shotgun and she walked through the field across from the farmhouse and she crossed the neighbor's field, and then the next one. Along the edge of the woods she saw a movement and a grouse flew up and Mae lifted the gun and pulled the trigger and the bird fell to the ground and Mae didn't feel sad because it was food and she thought of how good the meat would taste. At the edge of the cornfield she saw a woodcock but Gramps was next to her and said there's no meat and they taste wormy anyway, so she didn't shoot it. It wiggled its behind as its feet felt for worms, and she laughed and the woodcock thanked her for letting it go. The smell of leaves as they curled up and dropped to the ground was sweet and dry and dusty, and it was her favorite time of year and she was golden in the setting of the late afternoon sun, and as she carried the grouse back for Gram to cook, Mae felt happy and proud and responsible and good.

CHAPTER TWENTY-FOUR
Ruth, October 1943

"Let's get these birds into the air!" Martha yelled as she and Ruth and eight other women headed across the tarmac at Daugherty Field in Long Beach, California. The ten basic trainers, BT-13s, had to be ferried a few miles inland to Chino, and the women were looking forward to a short workday.

"Just a minute," one of the women shouted as she turned and ran back toward the administration building, "I forgot something. I'll be right back!"

"Wait, I'll come with you!" yelled another, running back with her.

"Should we get started?" Martha asked.

"No, let's wait for them," Ruth replied.

"Hey, Carole," said Martha to one of the others, "tell us again about your infamous landing in Georgia."

"Okay, Marth. Well, I was taking a Mustang from Palm Springs to Newark, and it was getting dark, and I decide to stop over in Georgia. So I start circling the Athens airfield and radioed the tower for landing instructions.

"So this guy gets on and says 'Lady, would you please get off the airwaves. We're trying to land a P-51.'

"So I look around for another P-51, and I don't see any, and I ask him again if I can land.

"So he comes on again, and he says, 'Listen, Lady! I need

you to get the fuck off the airwaves because I've got a fucking plane to put down.'

" And I say right back to him, 'Listen, Buster, the F-ing plane you have to land is mine! I'm running out of fuel and daylight and you're pissing me off!'

"So then I just say F it, and I make the dogleg, and I aim for the middle of the runway going like a bat out of hell, and I touch down and smoke the tires on the way in.

"Meanwhile the jackass in the tower is saying 'Great landing, man. Make sure you get your radio fixed, and boy, that landing was perfect!' He thought he was talking to the guy he couldn't make radio contact with!

"So I taxi up to the hangar and all these young guys in training are going gaga over the Mustang. So I freshen up my lipstick and brush out my hair and hop out onto the wing.

"It was so quiet you could hear a pin drop, and then they all start yelling and clapping and whistling at me! That guy in the tower must have felt like a real jerk.

"Well, let me tell you, I bet I had a really good time that night. I think I did. But I really can't remember!"

The group of women erupted into laughter. By then, the other two had returned and they headed for their planes. One by one, the trainers took to the sky.

The trip took less than 30 minutes, and one by one, they started to land. Ruth was the first on the ground. She taxied up to the hangar and hopped out of the cockpit. As the others came in, she stood on the side of the tarmac. One by one, five planes landed. The sixth was maneuvering the dogleg when it started to drop from the sky. Ruth and her companions watched in horror as the plane nosedived and disappeared behind the tree line at the end of the runway. Then they heard the explosion, and a plume of smoke rose into the air.

The women stared in shock at the black column billowing up from the trees and barely comprehended what they saw.

Then one of them said, "Who was it?"

Ruth's stomach dropped. Martha hadn't landed yet. Was it Martha? They were all friends. No matter who it was, it would not be okay, she knew that. In Ruth's mind, she knew that. But if it was Martha, if it was Martha . . .

Stunned, the women began to take a grim tally. Three planes had yet to come in.

The first landed and taxied to line up with the others. The pilot emerged from the cockpit. It wasn't Martha. There was a gasp of relief from one of the women, whose wish had been as fervent as Ruth's for her own best friend.

The next trainer landed. Ruth reached into her trouser pocket and closed her fingers around the silver dollar. It seemed to take forever until the plane finally parked and the pilot jumped to the ground. Again, it wasn't Martha.

Ruth's heart pounded. By now, the two pilots who'd just touched down had joined the group. They described the terror of seeing the aircraft go down in front of them and the carnage they'd flown over to reach the landing strip. But Ruth barely heard them. She was on the verge of tears as the last plane came in. Its wheels touched down. It taxied to the row of trainers and stopped. Ruth held her breath. Her fingernails dug crescents into her palm around the old coin. A moment later, Martha descended from the plane. Ruth choked a sob back into her throat, then breathed again.

The women looked at each other. Who had been in that plane? Who had they started out with, who hadn't landed? Virginia. Their friend Virginia.

The women staggered in shock to the administration building as firetrucks and army vehicles screamed to the scene of the crash.

CHAPTER TWENTY-FIVE

Mae, October 2020

A week after she'd received the letter from the lawyers, Mae remembered the note from Buddy. *Check out Gram's cedar trunk in the attic.* Mae headed up the stairs.

At nearly eight months pregnant, getting into and then out of the attic would be tricky. Mae looked at the doorway and considered her options. The best solution was to carry a kitchen chair up the stairs to the landing, climb onto it, and enter the small opening on her hands and knees. Mae moved carefully and deliberately, surprised that her heavy body still managed to execute the fairly athletic maneuver. Once inside the attic, she turned on the bare lightbulb and opened the cedar chest beneath it.

An old red cardboard box tied with a white ribbon sat on top of some of Gram's hand-knitted mittens and scarves. A yellow sticky note on the top of the box said "Mae." She picked up the box, along with a blue scarf. *Gram made this*, she thought. She closed the chest and turned off the light. She approached the door with some trepidation, trying to figure the best way to get her body out of the doorway and onto the chair. She sat down, held onto the door frame with one hand, and reached one foot out to the chair. Mae scooched herself forward, placed the box on the attic floor behind her, and turned around. She placed her other foot on the chair and pushed off, precariously unbalanced. She bent down and grabbed the chair with both hands. It worked. The chair stayed put. Mae step-hopped off the chair onto the stair landing, put the box and scarf on the seat of the chair, and pulled the door closed.

Damn, that was harder than I thought it would be.

Getting the chair back down the stairs was almost as hazardous as climbing in and out of the doorway. Halfway down, one of the legs caught on the railing and Mae stumbled forward. Her hand closed on the bannister and she recovered her balance. The scarf landed on the stairs. The box flew through the air and landed upside down on the living room floor. The chair bumped its way down the steps and settled next to the box.

Holy shit, she thought. Her arms instinctively wrapped around her bulging abdomen and hugged the baby inside her. Tears came to her eyes.

I am so sorry, little one, she whispered. *I've got to be much more careful with you.*

Mae held the railing tightly until she reached the bottom, then gingerly carried the chair to the kitchen, then retrieved the scarf from the stairs and the box from the living room floor and took them to the kitchen.

Still shaken by the near-accident, Mae fixed a cup of tea, then approached the box on the table. She sat in front of it, wondering why and how a box with her name on it was inside Gram's old attic trunk. How had Buddy known it was there? How had he known she'd be at the house? How had Gram known Mae would end up there? Was it even from Gram?

Mae took a breath and untied the ribbon. She removed

the lid and looked inside. A stack of paperwork filled the box. Flipping through the contents, she saw a scrapbook, some newspaper clippings, a photo album, and some official-looking documents.

Mae took the old handmade scrapbook from the box. The front said "Dear Milkman." Dozens of notes were glued to the pages. One said "Please don't leave any more milk until we come home again." Some of the notes were illegible, some were comical, many were illustrated.

Mae looked back into the box and removed a sheet of paper.

It was a letter from the Army Air Forces in Fort Worth, Texas. It was addressed to Ruth Franckling, Woodstock, New York, and was dated November 6, 1942.

Wait, thought Mae, *that's Gram!*

> Dear Miss Franckling:
> Thank you for your letter of November 2, 1942.
>
> Your application for admission to the Women's Flying Training course was received and from the facts stated therein it would appear that you are qualified for training.
>
> However, all applicants are subject to a personal interview by me, or some person I may designate, and to an Army physical examination.
>
> In the very near future we are planning to

have a recruiting officer somewhere in your vicinity at which time we shall notify you in order that you may arrange for a personal interview.

Yours very truly,
Jacqueline Cochran
Director, Women's Flying Training

Mae sat back and tried to absorb what she'd just read. This letter was addressed to Gram, when she was . . . what? 18, 19 years old? From the United States Army? The Army Air Forces. Mae had never heard of them. And writing to Gram about flying? Flight training? Mae could not make any connection between Gram and this letter dated nearly 80 years ago. There was no thread of association that made any sense to her.

Puzzled, Mae reached back into the box. She pulled out a small greeting card with a tiny red, white, and blue ribbon that read:

You've Earned Your Wings
Congratulations and Best Wishes

Inside was a poem about wings and "hoping that the best of luck will always fly with you," and it was signed "From the Mother's Guild."

Next came a pile of newspaper columns from further back in time. Mae had to look at several of the clippings before she figured out that Mr. Hasbrough was the owner of the Kingston airport and had written a regular column for the area newspaper. One of his favorite subjects seemed to be his newly hired pilot, Ruth Franckling, whom he called the Dawn Patrol. As she read, Mae's mind filled with images of a young woman in a leather helmet and goggles, a cream-colored silk scarf streaming out behind her as she soared through the sky. The columns spoke of her quick-thinking ability, an inherent instinct for aviation, and her seemingly natural set of flying skills.

Mae dug through the box and grabbed the black cardboard photo album. It was full of small black-and-white photographs with white scalloped edges, their corners glued to the black paper pages with little golden triangles.

The first photo was of a five- or six-year-old girl sitting inside what looked to be a homemade airplane fashioned from a wagon, complete with wings, a propeller, and paper streamers.

That must be Gram! A hundred years ago! Mae thought. *Wow. She must have always known she'd be a flyer!*

Mae turned page after page of photos of Gram at flight school, walking across an air base with friends. Rows of women pilots dressed in khaki pants and white button-down shirts, rigidly standing in straight formation lines with elbows out and hands held to their temples in salute. Mae gazed at the photos. Clear-eyed, young, confident faces gazed back at her. Most often, the familiar face, even at such a young age, the face that was Gram's. The smile had never changed through the years. The piercing eyes that always seemed to be looking farther ahead. So much about this young woman was familiar, and then Mae realized why. Every morning when she looked in the bathroom mirror, this was the face that looked back.

In amazement and admiration, Mae turned the pages, absorbing the visual narrative of Gram as a young woman. Sitting on the hood of a 1941 Packard. Looking to the sky, leather helmet and goggles perched on her head and brown bomber jacket zipped high against a cold morning. Striding across the tarmac toward a sleek, single-seater plane with a bold star painted on its side. Gram's handwritten caption read *Best of all—P51 Mustang.*

Another face frequented the photographs, someone who must have been special to Gram. Several shots of them together at different air bases. Romulus, Michigan. Great Falls, Montana. San Berdoo, California. Gram had written hasty captions on some of them: *Martha in front of our cottage. Martha all dressed up for flying in a PT—how do you like the boots? Me and Martha before horseback riding.* On one, a photo of a sunny leg on a lounge chair beside a swimming pool: *Martha, Palm Springs.* The last photo was taken from a cockpit with a wing in the foreground and a second plane some distance off to the left: *Martha and me headed east, October, 1944.*

Next from the box was an old cartoon of a mischievous-looking, impish girl with wings. She wore blue goggles and a yellow helmet with two little white horns on the top.

She had on a red dress, yellow tights, and red boots. She appeared to be landing, and the blue feathers of her wings trailed out behind her. Mae thought the cartoon seemed familiar, and when she read the signature, she knew why. The artist was Walt Disney. This cartoon of the flying girl with wings reminded her of the cartoons—the old Walt Disney movies—she'd watched with Buddy when she was little.

In the bottom of the box, Mae found two accounts of the demise of the WASP, the Women's Airforce Service Pilots. One was an article by Gill Robb Wilson, lamenting the congressional vote that ended the essential program, influenced by men who lobbied against the women pilots.

Another was a transcript from radio broadcaster Robert St. John, on December 20, 1944.

"Today is a mighty sad day," he began, and he proceeded to tell the story of the founding of the WASP and the amazing service record of more than a thousand women who flew more than 75 million miles between factories and air bases. Their error record was one-seventh that of the men's. They flew for $3,000 a year—a fraction of what men were paid, and they had no government pensions, no military status, no insurance for the next-of-kin of the handful of women who lost their lives performing this labor of love. No closing ceremony to honor them for their service, to thank them, to show them any appreciation for a truly exceptional job that was very well done.

The last item in the box, under all the papers, was a large, heavy coin. Mae picked it up and examined it. Its edge was battered, and the outlines were hard to see, as though they'd been worn down from continued rubbing. But Mae could discern, above the year, 1922, the profile of a female face, a beautiful, confident young woman whose thick, wavy hair was swept back. Tendrils flowed freely around her face.

She looks fearless, Mae thought. *I bet Gram looked like this when she was young: beautiful and fearless. I wonder where it came from. It must have been important to Gram, but why?*

Mae had to take a break. Sensory and information overload was giving her a headache and left her feeling short of breath. She pulled on Oma's old boots and barn jacket and headed outside. The sky was gray, but blue promised to poke through where the clouds were breaking up. She wandered down the driveway toward the mailbox and thought about the crazy morning she'd just experienced.

Oh, Gram! How did I not know any of this about you? Who were you, really? I thought I knew you, but I didn't. Why did you deliberately keep this from me? From us?

Mae's head felt ready to explode. She was in total awe of her great-grandmother and at the same time felt betrayed, let down, that none of this had ever been confided to her. She felt that she'd never been given the chance to know Gram, not really, and now it was too late.

But still. Still.

Jesus, Mae, she thought. *How about you don't make this about you? How about you think about Gram, and what it must have cost her not to tell you? To keep it all to herself?*

Certainly, if Gram had told anyone about it, everyone would have known. She must have kept it a secret.

Mae checked the mailbox. No mail. She started back to the house. The walk felt good and was beginning to clear her head.

The farm had always meant Gram and Gramps. The flavor, the fragrance of the farm had always been pie and lilacs and dirt and manure. The odors of springtime mud and sharp pickling vinegar in the fall. Sweet, ripe apples and the cows in the barn. Always Gramps and Gram in the background, always the essence of the farm.

Now a new aspect, a new feature emerged. A distant and ancient ingredient that changed its flavor. And would enhance it, Mae suspected, once she had time to digest it. And learn it. She had just grazed the surface of this overwhelming discovery; she didn't know if she was ready for more.

Back at the house, Mae made a sandwich and sat down at the table to continue through the box. The remaining newspaper clippings were from farther back in Gram's past.

Reading through Mr. Hasbrough's columns was time-consuming, but very interesting. One was about Gram becoming the first woman in the county to earn her commercial pilot's license in 1941.

Another told of the yearly trips from New York to Florida in the fall, then from Florida back to New York in the spring. Gram and another pilot would ferry Mr. Hasbrough's planes between the northern and southern airports.

Another column praised Gram's work as a flight instructor.

Damn, thought Mae. *There is so much more to Gram's life than I ever imagined. That she'd spent winters in Florida would have been a shock, let alone that she was flying freakin' airplanes there and back. And she was a flight instructor! At barely 18 years old!*

Mae suddenly felt like a slacker. In her twenties, she was a passenger in life, while Gram, at 17, had literally been flying the plane.

This time, when Mae called Oma's number, she vowed to herself that she would hang up if Maggie's answered. It wasn't Maggie. This time it was Buddy, and Mae melted at the sound of her grandfather's voice.

"Oh, Buddy, I haven't talked to you in so long! I miss you so much . . . "

"Maefly! It's so good to hear you! How are you? Are you doing okay up there on your own?"

"Oh, Buddy. There's so much to tell you but I'm doing good. I'm fine, I really am, but the house—Gram left it to me! And Gram, Buddy, the box! Her flying history! Wha—how, I mean, why didn't anyone ever tell me?"

"Oh, Mae. I'm sorry we never told you. Oma is out with Maggie right now, but I'll tell her you called and she has all the answers, Maefly. It's better if she tells you."

"I miss you so much, Buddy. I miss you and Oma so much."

CHAPTER TWENTY-SIX

Wesley, October 2020

The fender on James's pickup banged back and forth as the truck turned from the main road and came up the driveway. Mae smiled as Wesley and Jack tumbled out of the passenger side and tore across the lawn. The driver's door creaked open. James's lanky frame unfolded from the truck.

"Mae, can I leave Wesley with you today? I have to finish splitting a load of wood and deliver it to Fremont. Wes is bored anyway, and I won't have time to give him lunch, so can he and Jack stay here?"

"Of course, James! We always have fun, don't we, Wesley? We'll find something to do. Take as long as you need." Wesley erupted into a joyful shriek and ran around the yard. Jack barked and bounced up and down alongside him.

James yelled thanks as he climbed back into the truck, gunned the engine, and headed down the driveway.

"All right, Mr. Wesley, what shall we do today?" Mae asked as she walked toward the barn. "Would you like to ride the bike?"

Wesley ran into the barn and wheeled it to her. Mae steadied it while he climbed on, then he started pedaling and she let go. Once he had momentum, Wesley stayed balanced and steered toward the driveway. "Let's see if there's any mail, Wes," said Mae, and the three of them made their way up the lane. At the mailbox, Jack crossed in front of the bicycle. Wesley slowed and the bike tipped. Mae caught him just as he started to fall. He looked embarrassed.

"Wesley, you are doing great!" Mae fussed over him.

Wesley suddenly puffed up and felt very proud of himself. Mae always made him feel good.

He perched on the tips of his toes and peeked into the mailbox.

"Nothing!" he yelled.

"I guess we're too early," said Mae. "Do you want to go up to the Allen farm? We could see if they have any baby calves."

"Yay, calves!" Wesley shouted.

"All right, but let's walk, okay? We can leave your bike here for now. It's a little too far for you to ride just yet."

They turned up the main road and walked along the shoulder next to the stream. The day was cool and overcast, but walking warmed them. At the wide bend in the road, they spotted a deer carcass in the ditch.

Wesley ran over to inspect it.

"Wow."

"Yeah, wow!" said Mae. "I guess it was crossing the road and someone must have hit it with their car. Oh, look, Wesley, here's some broken glass from the headlight."

They looked at the dead deer for a while. Wesley picked up a stick and poked at it. Jack smelled around the carcass, but then got bored and headed into the bushes, and they continued up the road.

Mrs. Allen was leaving the milk house when they got to the

farm. She ducked back in and emerged carrying a plate that smelled wonderful.

"Here you go, Wesley! I bet you like peanut butter cookies. I just brought these down for Casper but he sure doesn't need all of 'em. And if you go up to the calf barn, you can see two new little heifers. Let me get some bottles of milk and you can feed them."

Wesley lifted the mask from his mouth and shoved in a cookie.

"Yummy!" he mumbled through the crumbs.

Up at the calf barn, Mae and Wesley found the two black and white calves in a little pen. A row of larger pens contained bigger calves that were munching on feed in the buckets that hung before them, and on hay that was spread on the floor.

The older calves could feed themselves, but the littlest ones still drank milk and had to be hand-fed.

"Here you go, Wesley!" Mrs. Allen handed him one bottle and gave the other to Mae. "Now, let the calf find the nipple, and tip up the end of the bottle so the calf gets milk instead of air. Hold on tight, because they'll pull the bottles right out of your hands."

Mae's little calf sucked earnestly, pulling the bottle forward with each gulp. The bottle ebbed back with each release. Mae remembered this as one of her favorite things about farm life.

Wesley's calf drank fast, and when the bottle was empty, the sucking sloshy sound of milk became hollow and full of air. Mrs. Allen helped Wesley pull the nipple from the calf's mouth, and Wesley laughed when it sucked on his fingers instead.

"That tickles!" he giggled, and Mae remembered her joy as

a little girl when she'd first felt the same sensation. She knew this would be a special memory for Wesley.

When her calf had finished drinking, Mae extracted the nipple from its mouth and handed the empty bottle to Mrs. Allen.

"I haven't done that for a very long time, Mrs. Allen. Thank you so much for letting us feed your calves; if it's okay with you, we'd like to come back and do it again sometime. And Pirate Wesley, I think lunch is waiting for us. Let's head back to the house. You can check the mailbox again, okay?"

They walked down the road, absorbed in their own thoughts while Jack trotted in and out of the bushes.

"Mae," asked Wesley, "what happened to the calves' mommies?"

"They live in the big barn with the other cows."

"But why don't they live with the calves?" Wesley's voice was pitched high and filled with concern.

Damn, thought Mae, *I didn't see this coming.*

"Well, Wesley, that's how it is on a dairy farm. In order to make milk, the mommies have their babies. Then the farmer takes over the job of feeding the babies, and the milk from the mommies is the milk we buy in the store. It's for us to drink."

As she explained it, she realized how ridiculous it must sound to Wesley.

"But that's not right!" Wesley's voice was a full octave higher. "And don't the calves ever get to see their mommies?"

"Well, yes, Wesley, they'll see them again. Since they live on the same farm, they'll get to be together after they have their own babies. Then they'll go into the big barn with their mommies."

"But that's a long time!" wailed Wesley, close to tears.

"They miss their mommies!"

Oh, man, thought Mae, *I should have thought this through. Of course he'd think of his own mother! I should have realized how sensitive this is. Shit!! What can I say to make him feel better?*

They had reached the wide sweep of the road and were almost at the deer carcass when they heard a large truck coming toward them. The truck came into view around the bend and seemed to be going too fast to make the curve. Mae grabbed Wesley's hand and frantically glanced around for Jack as she steered Wesley to the ditch along the side of the road. Beyond the ditch was a line of thick brush; they wouldn't make it to the opening into the field before the truck reached them.

It should be slowing down, Mae thought. *We have to get off the road. And where is Jack?*

Wesley's legs were rooted in place, even though he knew he had to run. The truck was barreling down on them, and Mae was dragging at his arm. He stared at the truck as it got closer and closer, fascinated by the sheer power of the speeding vehicle. Suddenly he felt his body being lifted into the air, and then he was in Mae's arms and they were hurtling into the bushes along the side of the road. Mae landed on her back on the ground. Wesley heard an "Oomph!" as his full weight landed on her soft, big belly.

Wesley peered into Mae's face. She peered back at him. Their masks had ripped away and their faces were flecked with blood from being scraped and poked as they'd plunged through the thorns and branches.

"Are you okay, Wesley?" Mae asked. He nodded yes.

"A-are you okay, M-mae?" Wesley asked in a voice that was small and fearful.

"Yes, Wesley, I think so," she said. "Let me move around a little so I can tell."

Wesley rolled off her and under a bush. He clambered to his hands and knees, never taking his eyes off her.

Mae took a couple of deep breaths. Nothing hurt bad. She rolled onto her side and got her knees under her. Her right elbow was really sore where it had slammed into the ground. She slowly stood up. A bruise here and there, maybe, but no real pains. Most important of all, the baby seemed okay, in spite of Wesley landing on top of her. Her body seemed to have adequately protected two little lives.

"I think I'm all right, Wesley!" she said in relief.

Mae was shaking, though, from fear, and anger, and the shock of how dangerously close the truck had come to her and Wesley. The driver must have seen them, but hadn't even slowed down. And Jack! Where was Jack? If something had happened to Jack, Wesley would be absolutely devastated.

"Jack!" she yelled. "Ja-ack! Here, Jack!" She whistled. "Come on, Jack! Come on, boy!"

Wesley looked at her in alarm. The trauma of the truck bearing down on them, the last-second launch into the air, and now the realization that Jack wasn't with them were too much for him. But just as he felt tears coming to his eyes, there was a rustling in the bushes next to him.

Jack burst though the branches and jumped on Wesley, and the long tongue licked his face. Wesley threw his arms around Jack and buried his face in the dog's chest. Jack sat still and let Wesley recover. He knew what Wesley needed. Mae watched in relief and awe. With some wise and ancient instinct, the dog nurtured and took care of the boy.

CHAPTER TWENTY-SEVEN

Ruth, November 2020

Dear Mae,

I know you have questions.

Let me try to explain about Gram. It's complicated.

There was a sorrow in Gram that she didn't show. It happened a long time before you were born.

One day when I was about your age, I walked into the kitchen and Gram was sitting at the table with tears running down her face. She tried to hide her sadness when she saw me. I asked her what was wrong. At first she said it was nothing, but I kept at her. I couldn't let it go; something important was bothering her. I saw she was holding a letter, and she showed it to me. It was an invitation to a reunion of some kind. I asked her what it was, and she said, "I'm only going to say this once, and then we're never going to speak of it again. Right?" So I said yes, and this is what she told me:

Gram was smart and kept getting pushed into higher grades at school, and she graduated when she was 16. She wanted to have adventures, to do something fun with her life, and she decided to take flying lessons at the local airfield. She didn't have much money, so she traded working at the airfield for her lessons. She learned fast, and soloed when she was 17, and then got certified to be a flight instructor, and the airfield hired her. (You know this already from the papers you found.) Then she was lucky to be hired by the Army Air Forces to ferry airplanes from the factories to the airfields. (You read about that too.)

The point is, Mae, that those were Gram's best years. Those women pilots contributed to the war effort in a way that most people will never know about. More than a thousand women put their hearts and souls into flying for their country, and some of them died doing it. They made sacrifices, and they loved their work more than anything in the world. It was their life.

Then one day, they were dismissed without even a thank-you from the army. They tried to stay—offered to work for a dollar a year if they could just keep flying. They'd been allowed to taste something bigger than themselves. To contribute. To do a job that was important, vital even, to winning World War II. But the program was disbanded. Overnight, it was snatched out from under them. It was a slap in the face to them, an insult.

Mae, Gram loved that time more than life itself. More than Gramps or me or anything.

Gram returned to her old airfield in Kingston and took up instructing again. She loved it, of course, but it no longer held the excitement it once had. Something good came of it, though; that's how she met Gramps. After the war, he decided to take flying lessons and ended up with Gram as his instructor. The next year they were married and moved to the farm. And she stopped flying. She never flew again.

So she boxed up that part of her life and tucked it deep inside her heart. That part of her life went black. Like it never existed. And she never spoke of it to anyone. I think she figured if she talked about it, she wouldn't be able to handle it——talking would dredge up all of the highs and lows, the insult, the deep sadness within her, and she might not recover from it. So she chose to lock it away. Gram was a woman of resolve. You and I both got that from her, Mae. Stubborn. Once she decided on something, that was that. She made up her mind and never spoke of flying again. She gave the rest of her life to raising me and doing her part on the farm.

Except every few years she'd get an

invitation in the mail to attend a reunion of the women pilots. Most of the time, she told me, she threw the invitations away. Just seeing the envelope put her in a funk for days. But for some reason, this time she'd opened the envelope and read the invitation, and allowed herself to feel all the sorrow she'd pent up inside, and then she let it out, and she told me. And then she stopped crying, and then she threw the invitation away, and we never spoke of it again. Ever.

On the farm, she was always working, always cooking or in the fields, or in the barn with Gramps, or tending the garden or mending clothes and almost never had time to herself. But you know, Mae, I think Gram had a small chance to feel a little bit of the freedom she'd found as a pilot. Do you remember the old white jeep, and how on summer days she'd drive it down to the post office in Fremont? Sometimes her black dog would sit on the seat next to her, with his ears blowing in the wind?

Oh, yes, Oma, I do remember! thought Mae.

Well, I think that was the closest that Gram ever got to flying again. With the windshield down, maybe the sounds, the rush of the air, the solitude and the freedom made her feel the way flying did. I'm so glad she had that little bit to make her feel vital again, Mae, you know—vivacious and alive.

Mae, the closest I ever saw her get to opening up was when she'd call you Fifi.. You said you found the drawing in the box she left you. Walt Disney drew that just for them, Mae! Fifinella was the mascot of her flying group. She was the playful little gremlin the pilots blamed all their mishaps and engine troubles on. And she represented their adventuresome spirits, their beautiful, youthful souls, and embodied their mission, their aspirations and ambitions.

I think she must have seen those bits of Fifinella, and of herself, in you. She saw hope, like maybe one day you'd get something like that of your own; a life bigger than yourself. Her eyes sparkled whenever she called you Fifi..

Mae, I hope you don't resent Gram, or me, from keeping this from you. It was what she wanted, and it was her secret to keep. But she wanted you to find out, eventually. Otherwise she wouldn't have kept that box of treasures in the attic. Right before she died, she made Buddy promise that you would find it. Now you know how much more there was to Gram, and also how much she loved you.

So now you know. Why she hid a huge

part of herself, why she left everything to you, and I think what her vision might have been for you. I don't think she ever cared what you do, sweetie, just that you do <u>something</u>, and whatever it is, it has to be something you love to do.

I hope this explains a lot. I hope you know how much we all love you.

I miss you so much sweetie.

Love,
Oma

CHAPTER TWENTY-EIGHT
Wesley, November 2020

Wesley's dad was talking to some men outside with a big log truck. They were trying to figure something out. Something about the timber at the top of the ridge, and how steep the mountain was on this side. They weren't happy with the owner, something about he needed it done fast and didn't care what it took. Wesley's dad said, "Okay, if you need to come down this way, you can," and then they started talking about where to put the logs.

Wesley and Jack got bored listening to the conversation and walked down the road to the bridge. Wesley picked up pebbles and tossed them into the stream below. Jack plunged into the chilly water to chase them, but Wesley stopped and just looked at the water. He missed playing the stick game with Luis. Thinking of Luis made him sad. He missed his friend. He missed his big smile and friendly eyes, and he missed hearing the funny way Luis talked.

The wind picked up. Wesley pulled his winter hat down over his ears, and he and Jack made their way back up the road toward the house. The big log truck came barreling past, much faster than it should have. The swirling dust encompassed them even though they'd moved off the shoulder of the road.

"I don't like those guys," Wesley said to Jack. "They seem mean."

The next day, Chester Destry drove his truck up Bearpen Road, west of the Welby valley, and parked at the base of the mountain. Chester unloaded the log skidder and started the long, slow trip up to the top on an old and overgrown logging road. The cold November rain turned to a light snow as the morning wore on.

Chester's father had purchased the old skidder in 1967. It served him well until one day in 1994 when he was working an oak stand near Walton. A falling oak had dislodged a widow maker—a dead limb hanging from a nearby tree—that broke off and landed on him. Chester had been downhill and heard the crash. He'd run up and discovered his father's body. The limb had crushed his chest and pinned him to the ground.

Chester took over the operation. His two-man logging enterprise included his poorly-paid cousin Silas and depended both on swindling property owners and encroaching on neighboring lands, state-owned or privately held, to harvest any desirable timber in sight. His equipment was run hard and minimally serviced. Needless to say, it had aged neither gracefully nor safely.

The prize oak trees Chester now sought behind the Hubbard place grew just down from the top of the ridge near severe ledge rock. Because their natal acorns had come to rest and sprouted on one of the steepest escarpments in the Catskills, the oaks had been sheltered and protected from timber harvests. For a hundred years, the oaks had grown from seedings to saplings and, finally, into strong and sturdy colossals. In the past 50 years, they had begun to reproduce, releasing legions of acorns to the slopes beneath.

The landowner wanted the oak sold as soon as possible. The COVID economic downturn had decimated his business, and harvesting the huge, valuable trees was the only possible way he figured he could stay afloat. He told Chester that the quicker he could get them out, the bigger his bonus. Which is why Chester and Silas asked James for permission to come down off the ledges behind the house and to build a log landing just behind the barn; from the ledges, there was no way to get back up. Chester would pull the logs off the mountain and his cousin would load them onto the truck and haul them to the lumberyard.

Chester finally got the skidder to the top of the mountain. He crested the ridge, spit an impressive amount of brown, gooey saliva into his can, stuck another slug of tobacco into his cheek, and pointed the skidder down the mountain. He aimed for the top of the ledge rocks, figuring he'd back off across from the ledges as soon as he'd cleared his way to the oaks, park the skidder for the night, and bushwhack over to the old deer trail that meandered down the mountain. It'd take him about forty-five minutes to meet up with Silas behind the Hubbard place. They'd start logging tomorrow.

He'd taken machinery up and down the steep valleys of the Catskills since he could remember, giving him the confidence it took to accept this job. Confidence, along with more than a little overblown bravado. But this descent was more severe than he'd ever faced before, and an inch of snow covered a layer of ice that had formed on top of the exposed rock surfaces. Sweat broke out down his back and across his brow. The skid steer was old. He'd kept it going for a long time, and he hoped it was up to this. He hoped *he* was up to this.

Chester creaked the machine down the steep slope. The big, chain-clad wheels churned over shrubs, bushes, and small trees. He'd been at this work for most of his life, and he had a feel for it. He could pretty much tell the lay of the land by the way the vegetation grew, and he could sense the limits of the machinery. But the problem with working this high up was that you couldn't always see the drop-offs. Sometimes vegetation hid fissures in the ledges. And if you got in trouble with ledges, then the limitations of the machinery didn't matter at all.

Over to his right was the oak stand, above the other trees. It was time to turn across the slope. "Goat slope" is what they called it. More treacherous when it was covered with ice and snow.

A person shouldn't even be on this slope, let alone try to drive equipment across it, he thought. That's why the oaks had lasted as long as they had—no one had dared to go after them.

Screeching and grinding its way across the mountain, the skidder made a terrible racket.

Wesley and Jack had walked back to the house and were poking along the little stream. Jack suddenly looked toward the mountain and started barking. Seconds later, Wesley heard a groan and a squealing sound coming from the mountain. He looked up in horror. He was terrified. The giant had never been this close to the house before. It had always been across the valley. Wesley had always thought he would hear it in time.

It's coming! The COVID is coming! was all he could think.

Wesley ran to the barn, looking for his dad. He called out; there was no answer. His heart racing, he ran to the back of the barn. His dad's truck was there, but he wasn't around! Could the COVID have gotten him already?

More shrieking rang down from the mountain.

James and Silas stood at the recently cleared log landing on the rise behind the barn. They could hear the skidder up on the ridge.

"Why the hell are you guys after that oak anyway?" asked James. "It's gonna be shit to get out, you know."

"Oh, we know that," said Silas. "But we couldn't turn down the money. The guy's seein' a gold mine in them trees. We didn't have the heart to tell him that a lot of those oaks is already rotten."

The men stood still and listened to the drone of the skidder as it began to work its way down the mountain.

"You know, this isn't what we agreed on," said James. "You're too close to the stream. You got dirt pushed into the water." They looked down at the fresh pile of mud that nearly blocked the little creek and turned the clear, clean water thick and brown.

"I don't give a flyin' fuck." said Silas. "We'll be outta here in a month, and then you can do whatever you want with it."

"I think you're gonna fix it before you leave," said James,

"or you'll be in deep shit. And by the way"—he eyed Chester's cousin warily—"did you guys do that clear-cut beyond the Griffin place?"

"We sure as hell did," said Silas. "We got paid good money for it, too."

"Well, yer assholes," said James, "You did a fuckin' shit job, and you should be ashamed of yerselves."

They both looked up as a God-awful screech rang down from the mountain.

It was all Chester could do to work the directional levers and keep the skidder moving straight. The weight of the machine was fighting the pitch of the mountain, and the mountain was winning. The skidder was screaming. More sweat ran down Chester's face and neck. He chewed hard at the plug of tobacco in his cheek.

The control lever jumped from his left hand as some ledge rock crumbled under the front tire. All at once there was nothing but air where there should have been rock. Chester yanked the right lever, fighting to pull the skidder back from the edge.

Ah, fuck, he thought. *Goddamn it, I'll die on the mountain just like my fuckin' dad. Shit, I didn't want it to happen today. Fuck, I'm not ready to die.*

More of the sandstone ledge collapsed, this time under the skidder's rear tire, and Chester felt the machine shift as the left side dangled precariously from the edge. Then the skidder groaned and tipped and spun off the side of the mountain into nothing. First he was sideways, then upside down, then right side up, then he was thrown from the cab as the skidder tumbled end over end down the sheer cliff face. He had probably been knocked unconscious, probably hadn't felt his head smack into the oak tree on the side of the mountain, the oak that crushed his brain; the oak they found his body crumpled beneath, hours later.

The skidder rolled and bumped and slid down the mountain, snapping trees like toothpicks, creating a swath that was visible from the main road.

As the violent noise echoed down the mountain, Wesley frantically searched for his father. He was nowhere to be found. Wesley ran shrieking toward the pond.

It was after him. It had gotten his dad.

He had no defense; no spears, no rocks. His COVID mask was in his room, on his dresser. He hadn't thought he'd need it when he played so close to home.

Wesley was barely cognizant that Jack was running beside him. The dog was alert but confused by the shroud of panic emanating from his boy. Jack was prepared to attack. He understood nothing that was happening except his job: to protect Wesley.

Wesley's throat was sore, his shrieks barely louder than a whisper. His brain no longer processed. His body would run as long as it could. Until it couldn't.

Wesley felt his legs give way as he neared the pond. He hit the ground hard, the air instantly forced from his lungs. He was crying and gasping and wheezing, trying to inhale, when a hand reached out and grabbed his arm.

Wesley screamed again, certain that the COVID had caught him. Then he felt his father's strong arms around him, rocking him back and forth, back and forth, as light snow feathered down on the boy and his dad and the dog that trembled next to them. James rocked and rocked his son, while Wesley sobbed and sobbed and sobbed until there were no tears left to cry.

CHAPTER TWENTY-NINE

Mae, November 2020

Oh, damn, she thought. *I guess I'd better get a phone.* Now that she had some money, Mae could afford to have the phone company hook up the landline. The old black dial phone was still in the closet. Two weeks away from her due date, Mrs. Allen had told her the birth could happen anytime. And although Lanore was faithful, checking on her every morning, Mae thought she should probably have a phone in case things started to happen during the night.

Mae grabbed her backpack and started for the Allen farm. She could call the phone company from there and would pick up some more eggs and a quart of milk. She had stopped riding her bike two weeks before, and she was trying to walk for an hour every day.

Mae was tired. She hadn't been sleeping well. The baby kicked a lot and allowed her only short catnaps during the night.

By the time she reached the farm, Mae was exhausted. The walk took more out of her than she'd anticipated, and she thought maybe she should ask Mrs. Allen for a ride home.

In the milk house, she pulled two egg cartons and a bottle of milk from the refrigerator, put them in her backpack, and placed twelve dollars in the Tupperware. She walked up to the house and knocked on the door. There was no answer. Mae walked back down to the barn. It was all strangely quiet;

no one was around. Patsy's car and Casper's truck were both gone.

What the heck? Mae thought. *Someone's always here.*

She started the long walk home. With each step, her body felt heavier. Her head felt light.

Oh, shit, she thought. *Low blood sugar. Forgot to have breakfast.*

She heard a water truck speeding down the road behind her. She stepped off the shoulder into the field as the truck blasted past her and the wind tore at her scarf and hat.

Jesus, she thought. *I'm glad I wasn't on my bike.*

She finally made it to the mailbox and peered inside. Nothing. There was usually nothing, but she hadn't seen Lanore pass by, either. Strange, for a Tuesday.

Oh, Mae thought. *Tuesday. First Tuesday of November. Election Day.*

Mae headed down the driveway. With each step she was more uncomfortable. She was past exhaustion and in a daze as she entered the house, went straight to the bedroom, stepped out of her shoes, and dropped into bed. She fell asleep as her head hit the pillow.

Several hours later, Lanore banged on the door.

"Mae! Are you okay?" Lanore went around the back and looked in the kitchen window. She couldn't see anything indicating that Mae was home, and she had a strange feeling that something was wrong. She decided to go in. She opened the door of the mudroom, then barged into the kitchen. She heard gentle moaning off to the side.

"Mae!" she yelled. She burst into the living room and saw Mae on her hands and knees, rocking back and forth.

"What should I do, Mae? What do you need me to do? Oh Mae—I'm gonna go get Patsy! Do you need anything before I leave?"

Mae turned her head and mouthed "no." She was about to tell Lanore that Patsy wasn't home, but she'd already gone.

Jenny had dropped off a booklet called *How to Have a Baby at Home*. In it were instructions for everything from sterilizing baby clothes in the oven to tying off an umbilical cord with a clean shoelace. Mae had followed all the steps. She had baby blankets and towels ready. She had sheets and towels for the delivery ready. Mae figured she was as prepared as she could be for all manageable circumstances.

The book said, "You won't know what position you'll deliver the baby in until you deliver the baby! The right position is what feels comfortable. Women have delivered babies standing up, lying down, kneeling, and squatting. Just remember to catch the baby! It will be quite slippery, so try your best not to drop it." This was the only information Mae had to go by.

Mae had felt the pull before she processed the pain. Three hours after getting back to the house and crawling into bed, she'd awoken with contractions. She slowly got up and prepared for the birth. In between contractions, she made a pallet of blankets on the floor (to make a soft nest) and covered them with a tarp she'd found in the barn (because things would get messy) and then with clean, sterilized sheets (to keep the baby from getting germs). She had put on Buddy's big old tie-dyed shirt (because it was comfortable and made her feel loved) and had filled her water bottle and placed it within easy reach. When contractions hit, she made her way to the kitchen, leaned against Gram's sturdy wooden table, and breathed into the force and the pain. She was scared.

Oh, damn, Fifi, what did you get yourself into? How am I supposed to do this? I don't even know what I'm supposed to do. I'm freakin' alone and having a baby. I don't know what to do!

Tears spilled from her eyes and rolled down her cheeks. She breathed in as she felt another contraction hit.

Oh fuck oh fuck ohfuckohfuck!

In between the pain, she must have slept. She slept standing at the table, and dreamed that Gram and Oma were with her.

"It's okay, Fifi," Gram said. "You're not doing anything that dozens of women in our family haven't done before. You'll be fine. Your body knows what to do. You just have to let it. Go lie down and relax. It's almost done."

Mae roused and left the kitchen. She went into the living room and placed more wood into the stove, gulped some water, then lay down on the pallet she'd prepared. She rested between contractions. Then they got stronger.

She turned and raised herself to her hands and knees. As she rode the crest of each new round of pain, she rocked back and forth, back and forth, in a soothing and calming rhythm.

That's when Lanore had appeared, seen Mae in labor, and left.

Mae was in a daze. All her senses turned inward. She

heard and felt nothing except the pull on her body.

The baby moved downward. The contraction started as a dull ache, then throbbed to a peak, then abated. Oma and Gram must be in the room; Mae could hear murmurs and soft words and felt warm encouragement envelop her. The pain increased as her pelvic bones and ligaments moved and stretched; each contraction ripped and tore, then released a blinding bolt of pain. Over and over, the contractions pushed the baby farther along, then farther again. Mae rocked back and forth, back and forth. She groaned, then yelled, and finally screamed as each push required more and more effort, more energy than she had left. She was hoarse, she was exhausted. Then Gram's voice, "Lie down, lie down, you need to rest." Mae slowly turned to her side and lay down on her pallet and slept. One minute seemed like an hour, and then a contraction hit and she woke again with a wrenching, tearing sensation and felt an emergence between her legs. She reached down and felt a softball-sized, wet head in her hands. Her body pushed again, a tremendous push. "The baby," she heard Oma and Gram say softly, and Mae reached again and felt the head push forward, and the shoulders came out and there was a sliding of the little torso and it was almost too slippery to hold as it slithered toward the floor. But she had it! She pulled the little body up to her stomach and rested for a few minutes, then felt for for the bag holding the clean scissors and shoelace she'd placed near the pillow. With them, she tied a knot and cut the umbilical cord. The baby squirmed and mewed and snuggled against Mae's chest. Once again, contractions. Mae groaned and pushed and then the placenta was out. Finally, she pulled a blanket over the two of them and fell into a deep sleep.

The next time Lanore burst in, Mrs. Allen and Mariella were right behind her. The three of them tornadoed into the living room and stopped short at the sight of Mae and her baby resting in the tousled nest on the floor.

Mae opened her eyes.

"Can you all put masks on?" she asked weakly. "If you don't have one, there's some in a basket by the door."

The three women pulled on masks and moved to Mae's side.

"The baby! What a beautiful baby, Mae! Are you all right?"

Mae smiled and held the baby out for them to see.

"I'd like you to meet Fifinella McCain. I'm going to call her Fifi."

Mrs. Allen took Fifinella for a quick exam. Mariella started a pot of tea, while Lanore helped Mae to the rocking chair and cleared the bedding from the floor.

Then they gathered around Mae and the baby.

"I walked up to your farm this morning, Mrs. Allen," said Mae, "but no one was there, so I came home."

"Oh, sweetie," said Patsy, "I was at the Grange Hall today. I'm on the Board of Elections and we started this morning at five. I was sure you'd be okay—it's still almost two weeks until your due date. I'm so sorry!"

"And the substitute driver delivered the mail today because I had a dentist appointment this morning," said Lanore, "so I came up later, and that's when I found you in labor, so I went to get Patsy."

"When Lanore came into the Grange," Patsy said, "I could tell by her face that something was wrong, so I jumped up and ran out."

"I'd just finished voting," said Mariella, "so I came along to see if I could help."

"Mae, you did great," said Patsy. "But I'm so sorry you did this alone."

"But it didn't seem like I was alone," said Mae. "I could feel Gram and Oma with me the whole time. I could hear them. They told me I would be okay, and they helped me through the contractions. I lay down on the floor. I remember Gram saying to take it slow. So I pushed and pushed, and all of a sudden the baby came out. I put her on my stomach and we just lay there, resting, snuggled up under the blanket, and that's when you all came in."

"Beautiful," Mariella said. "This reminds me of life in my village in Mexico. It makes me miss my abuela."

Mrs. Allen jumped up.

"Oh, golly, I have to get back!" She headed for the door. "There are supposed to be three of us at the table, and when I left they had to close the polls. They put up a sign telling folks to come back later. Mae, I'll stop in on my way home tonight to check on you. Lanore, can you stay for a while and help Mae get into bed? Mariella, you can come with me now, or catch a ride back with Lanore, but I've gotta go."

After Mrs. Allen left, Mariella held and cuddled the baby on the couch while Lanore helped Mae into a warm shower, and then Lanore and Mariella took Mae and the baby to the bedroom.

Mae had emptied the bottom drawer of her dresser and lined it with soft blankets for the baby, but now she couldn't bear to give her up. Not yet. Lanore fluffed the pillows and settled Mae into bed, while Mariella placed the baby beside her.

"Let's see if she's ready to nurse," said Mariella. "Just put her here, this way, and try to get her to . . . there, see, she knows what to do! We'll be here if you need anything. You both are muy cansadas—very tired. You need your rest."

"You kind of remind me of Grace O'Malley," Lanore said to Mae. "She was an Irish pirate who had to fight marauders off her ship after she gave birth."

"I can't even imagine that," said Mae. "I just want to sleep."

"She did, too," said Lanore, "which is why the whole time she fought off the invaders she was bellowing at her crew for their incompetence. The raiders thought she was a ghost—a screaming banshee who'd appeared from nowhere, brandishing a very large sword. After the last of them jumped off her ship, she went back below decks to her newborn son and didn't emerge for two days."

"Why do I remind you of her?" asked Mae as she began to drift off to sleep.

"Because you're strong, Mae. Very strong."

Lanore and Mariella stepped out of the bedroom. Mariella assembled a pot of soup while Lanore put together a casserole from the contents of the cupboards and the refrigerator.

"Do you think we should tell her about the accident?"

"No, not today," said Mariella. "Let her have a beautiful day with her daughter, without any bad news at all."

Lanore agreed. There was no reason that Mae needed to hear about the tragedy on the mountain, the mangled log skidder behind the log landing and how Casper Allen had taken his tractor as far up as he could, Silas clinging to the side, and how they'd climbed their way on foot along the skidder's path of splintered trees until they discovered Chester's body lodged against the base of a towering oak.

Three and a half weeks later, Mae pulled a roast turkey from the oven and put rolls in to brown. She mashed a pot of boiled potatoes with a stick of butter, then turned off the burner under a frying pan full of string beans. She pulled a bowl of Gram's special cranberry sauce from the fridge and stirred the drippings from the turkey into a pot of gravy.

Fifinella was outdoors at the picnic table with James. Wesley stood at his dad's side, the patch covering his right eye and his left eye gazing at the little bundle of wonder in his father's arms, this tiny little baby. Would she really grow into a little girl? Would she really become big enough to chase frogs and wade in the crick and play with him? This was the first time he'd ever seen a baby this close. He felt he could look at her all day. He reached out to touch her tiny, perfect hand. She opened her gray-blue eyes and looked at him. Wesley felt his heart soften. Jack lay on the ground at their feet and his tail thumped with happiness at the feeling of content that surrounded his family. The constant strain he'd sensed in Wesley, and James, too, had melted away, replaced with a peace they hadn't felt since before Wesley's mother died.

"Earth to Wesley," James said softly. "Do you s'pose you could go ask Mae if she needs some help? I'd do it, but I've kinda got my hands full."

Wesley adjusted his face mask and scampered into the house.

"Mae, do you need some help?"

"Why, yes, Pirate Wesley!" she said. "Can you please put this cloth on the picnic table? Then come back for the plates and silverware?"

"Aye, aye, Captain Mae," he said, and he took the tablecloth outside.

Mae and Wesley successfully ferried the whole Thanksgiving dinner to the table. The late November day was chilly, and snow showers were forecast for later that night. But the afternoon sun was pleasant, and with winter hats and enough layers on, everyone was comfortable. It was the first time they'd been together since the logging accident, since the birth, and it felt like a real celebration to sit down together and share a meal.

"This wild turkey is fantastic, James!" said Mae, holding Fifi in the crook of her arm. "Thank you for contributing it to the feast."

"You cooked it just right, Mae. Some people leave it in too long and it dries out. You did it perfect."

Mae noticed that Wesley was kind of subdued and that he tended to stay near his dad's side; she thought it was probably a response to Chester Destry's death. In a way, she was right.

Mae wasn't aware of the trauma Wesley had suffered the day of Chester's death, the day of Fifi's birth. At bedtime on that tragic day, Wesley had rummaged in back of his closet and hesitantly given his dad the old T-shirt wrapped around the cache of knives. James had choked back his tears and hugged Wesley tight. The following day, Wesley led his dad to the little fort behind their house. Wesley had crawled in and, moments later, emerged with the hunting knife, tearfully apologizing, explaining that he'd needed it to sharpen his sticks. James tenderly gathered Wesley in his arms and sheltered him as the boy sobbed. Tears ran down James's face as he slowly rocked his son from side to side, and a subtle, subconscious tension between them was broken; the unacknowledged barrier of sadness between them had eased. Their healing had finally begun.

"Wesley, what do you think of Fifinella?" asked Mae.

"She's beautiful. I love her," Wesley answered, his voice low and catching in his throat. Mae and James smiled at each other in relief. Wesley was subdued, but he was whole. Whatever each of their concerns had been for the little boy, James and Mae both knew he was okay.

CHAPTER THIRTY

November 2025

Mae straightened up from the patch of greens she'd been working in. Her hand instinctively felt for the coin in her pocket. Fifinella ran to her with a basket of herbs she'd picked from her very own row. Ten other five- and six-year olds were picking and filling baskets from their rows, too.

Twelve elementary students were at the edge of the pond, studying aquatic insects. They pulled their nets from the water and splashed in their barn boots through the boggy ground that was just beginning to freeze up. They laughed and yelled as one of the boys chased the rest of them into the field. One of the girls headed for the porta-john behind the 80-foot-long greenhouse.

James came down the mountain path with the high schoolers. Seven boys and girls had just completed a tree and plant identification exam as they'd hiked from one end of the farm to the other.

Throughout the school year, even on snowy days, classes were held outdoors. Science and math lessons were abundant on the mountain and in the plant and animal life the youngsters studied in the stream, the pond, and the meadows. Once a week, the students went to the Allen farm and worked with Casper in the barn and in his fields.

In autumn months, the harvest from the greenhouse and the garden was shared with every family.

Today, the picnic tables had been placed end to end and all the students gathered for a harvest celebration. Mae and her little ones put bowls of fresh-picked greens on the tables.

"Look!" said one of the boys, pointing to the sky as several dozen geese honked overhead, heading south in V formation.

Mae sat between Jenny and James and watched the chatting and laughing students fill their plates with potatoes and squash and turkey that had been roasted in the fire pit. Everyone was adorned with a necklace or a headdress fashioned from tree bark, berries, or dried grasses.

"L is for *Lycopodia!*" Wesley declared with an easy smile as he came up behind Mae and gently placed a woven green circle on her head.

She watched the 11-year-old as he sat down among his friends and joined the conversations around him. The eye patch had done its job; his gaze was even and his self-confidence, obvious.

Across the table, Fifinella giggled with her friends as they somewhat accurately poured juice into each other's glasses. Her hair was thick and curly like Mae's and her smile was wide like Max's. Mae had told Max about Fifi after she was born. He'd visited them last year and was planning to come back in the spring. Fifinella's eyes, those bright blue eyes, danced and sparkled whenever she got excited about anything, which turned out to be almost everything. They were Gram's, and Oma's, eyes.

Mae thought about the trajectory her life had taken. She lived in the house that had always felt like home, she had birthed little Fifi, and she and Jenny together had started this wonderful school. Mae was grateful that James had accepted the teaching position; he and Wesley finally had financial stability and James had made some repairs to the cabin. Best of all, he'd met Joanie, the mother of one of the younger students. They'd been spending lots of time together, and both James and Wesley seemed happy and settled.

Changes had occurred in the valley, as well. The water bottling plant was shut down after the OSHA investigation of Luis's death. Once again, the loudest sound in the valley came from the tractor going from Casper's barn to the fields. And now Mae and Fifi and Wesley could safely ride their bikes up the road to visit the calves.

Oma and Buddy would be coming for a couple of weeks at Christmas. Oma said that Maggie was doing better, but she didn't want to leave her for very long.

I've come so far from the night I walked into Gram and Gramps's deserted house five and a half years ago, Mae thought. *After feeling alone and off course for so long, I'm exactly where I want to be.*

Mae looked up at the sound of a small plane overhead. Maybe it was Gary. After he returned to New York, he'd sold his apartment, moved upstate, and earned his pilot's license. Sometimes he landed his little Carbon Cub on one of Casper's fields and took Mae and Fifi over the farm. They'd fly above the patchwork of woods and fields, then follow the streams that rambled out of the mountains down along the valley floor to Fremont and beyond. Their conversations inevitably turned to Gram and her story. Maybe that's where Gary's love of flying came from. And Mae's. And Fifi's.

The plane turned eastward toward the barn and farmhouse.

Maybe it's Gram, thought Mae. She liked to imagine Gram piloting a P-51 above the forests and fields, eternally following rivers and railroads as far as she liked, then banking and diving and leveling off on new headings.

Maybe Gram was looking down at the farm she and Gramps had loved, and the new greenhouse, and all the students seated around the table, and maybe, just maybe, Mae could hear Gram's soft voice saying,

"You've got this, Fifi; you've found your wings. You've finally learned to fly."

Mae's hand felt for the precious coin in her pocket, the bumps and dents on its battered edge. Even through her jeans she thought she could make out the contours of the girl's face and hair.

Fifinella was intrigued by the coin; at bedtime she studied the face on the front and the eagle on the back. She had memorized every aspect, and together she and her mother had learned its history.

Her name was Teresa de Francisci. She was the wife of the coin's sculptor, who had agonized over the best image to commemorate the end of World War I. In the end, he had chosen the profile of his strong and independent young bride.

How perfect, Mae thought, *how very perfect. Teresa, Ruth, Oma, Mae herself, and now, Fifinella,* and their faces floated before her.

The wild, unruly tresses of us all, she thought, as she fingered the bumps and ridges of the battered old coin.

AFTERWORD

The accounts of my mother's flights are true and well-known in our family, and are told in this story as she had related them to me. Some details and backstory have been embellished for dramatic effect, but for the most part, the incidents occurred as they are written.

In 1941, Ruth was the first woman in Ulster County, New York to earn a commercial pilot license.

During the two years she served as one of the Women Airforce Service Pilots (Class 43-W-2), two of Ruth's aircraft malfunctioned, and only her quick thinking averted disaster.

One of her saddest memories was witnessing the crash that killed her friend, Virginia Moffett, on October 5, 1943.

Martha Wagonseil was Ruth's best friend for life. For years, Ruth and Martha attended WASP reunions held in various locations around the country.

Carole Fillmore wowed the guys at the Athens airfield when the air traffic controller refused to believe she was piloting the P-51. Growing up, I had often heard the story from my mother. In 1973, Carole related the account to me personally when Ruth, Martha, and I visited her in California.

In 1977, the WASP were awarded full military status, entitling them to military funerals.

In 2010, the WASP were presented the Congressional Gold Medal. My siblings and I attended the ceremony in Washington, DC, along with Martha's son and daughter.

Ruth really did say they were the best days of her life.

Ruth really did fly through a rainbow.

She met my father when she was his flight instructor. She and Gramps lived on the family farm for nearly 60 years.

My cousin Gary was inspired by my mother to become a pilot, and he graciously flew Ruth's ashes on a "final flight" over the farm on a sunny summer day in 2007.

More information on the WASP is available from the WASP Museum in Sweetwater, Texas, where Ruth's dress uniform jacket is on display, and the National Museum of the United States Air Force in Dayton, Ohio, which houses Ruth's bomber jacket and the kneeboard on which she jotted notes while flying her missions.

Except for Ruth's aerial adventures, the book is fictional, although many of the dream sequences relate events from my childhood.

Some of the characters are based on real family and community members or are amalgams thereof.

There really is a Lanore, who was our mail carrier and is as nice in person as she is in the book.

Our family keeps Ruth's battered silver dollar in a beautiful box along with an assortment of pins, medals, and memorabilia from her flying days.

ACKNOWLEDGEMENTS

Thank you, Kemp Battle, for guiding this book through the process that allowed it to be written, whether you knew it or not. Kemp, there's more to come.

Thank you, Karen Rauter for the first reading and encouragement. Thank you to Nancy Reynolds, my sister and cheerleader, who read and approved multiple changes and cuts.

Multitudinous thanks to Sharon Israel, for the comprehensive phone call Master Class. Thank you for seeing that the elements were there, and for telling me so. Your suggestions were essential.

Many thanks to Melissa Holbrook Pierson for your revision class and brilliant suggestions.

Thank you, Laurie Lieb, for the superb editing that made the book readable, and to Fabia Wargin for connecting us and for the beautiful cover design.

And thanks, not least, to my friend Leslie T. Sharpe, whose gentle exhortations keep me writing.

Thank you, my beloved Brigadoon: this book exists only because of our special valley and those who live here. We are an anachronism staring into the inevitable face of change. I hope you find recognition and amusement in these pages, and I hope I have offended no one in the license I have taken to craft the story. I love you all.

CPSIA information can be obtained
at www.ICGtesting.com
Printed in the USA
JSHW030128211022
31824JS00003B/45